Infinite Justice

Infinite Justice

by

J. J. Hunter

WORDS WORTH PRESS
Enterprise, Oregon

Published by
Words Worth Press
PO Box 398
Enterprise, OR 97828
(541) 426-6095

First Edition

Printed and bound in USA

ISBN: 0-915214-40-7

Dedication

My doctor the chef

J. J. Hunter is the pen name of the author

PROLOGUE

THIRTY-THREE YEARS EARLIER
THE CARIBBEAN ISLAND NATION OF TROPICAN

The little girl wailed as she clawed at the ropes that bound her mother and father in the living room of their small house. Her parents were tied back-to-back in two wooden chairs. Their mouths were taped so they could not speak or even kiss their little girl goodbye. Tears filled the eyes of the mother. Her proud father, blood oozing from wounds on his head, sat up straight and defiant.

"Sergeant Castille, I am almost ready," said the young Tropican soldier as he piled explosives under the chairs of the captives.

"Good. Hurry man, hook up the switch."

The child studied the face of the soldier and looked into his eyes as he attached the wire. He was trembling as he pressed the detonation button down with his thumb and attached the wires. "What about the little girl?" he asked.

"We'll take her with us so she can witness the fate of traitors to our glorious Prime Minister." Castille grabbed the girl, barely three feet tall, and held her at his waist. She kicked and screamed as he carried her outside.

The front door of the cottage flew open as the young soldier bolted from the house. He released the button and dropped the switch on the porch then dove for cover behind a concrete retaining wall between the house and street.

An enormous explosion rocked the dwelling from its foundation and pieces of the roof blew hundreds of feet in the air. The windows shattered and the walls caved in creating a gigantic inferno. The little girl went limp in the arms of Sergeant Castille and hung her head, overcome by the pain of watching the horrendous murder of her parents. Tiny Antoinette would remember this day and the faces of the assassins for the rest of her life.

CHAPTER ONE

KANSAS CITY, MISSOURI

Bob Robinson arrived for work in the gleaming Emrae International Tower Building thirty minutes before his shift. After forty years of service to the worldwide conglomerate, he had risen to his dream job in the company.

He entered the building through the employee entrance and waved to his friend Charlie in the security shack. Bob walked down two flights of stairs to the employee locker room where he changed into his uniform, put on polished black work shoes and pinned his name tag directly over his heart. He had one cup of black coffee in the employee break room and exactly at 10 PM punched his timecard and immediately began working.

Robinson was the senior custodian in the company's international headquarters building, which meant he was personally in charge of the cleanliness of the seventy-second floor of the skyscraper. This was the floor of the building where Chairman and CEO Curtis Sittinz was housed. The janitor pushed his cart to the service elevator and piloted it to the top floor.

He entered the door to the CEO's palatial office suite and walked past the administrative assistant's desk into the inner office. Bob went behind the executive's massive desk and picked up a gold-plated wastebasket to empty it, but as had been the case for many weeks, the can was empty.

Chairman and CEO Curtis Sittinz had been AWOL for over a month and nobody knew his whereabouts. Rumors had him hiding out in dozens of countries around the globe.

Emrae International was one of the world's biggest and most successful companies prior to Sittinz and his people taking control. His picture appeared on the covers of countless business publications and he was known throughout the world as a financial mastermind. Wherever he went reporters and paparazzi followed his every move.

On Labor Day weekend, the scandal broke. It became clear that instead of being the world's premiere businessman he was its biggest swindler. Along with a secret partner, he raped the company of its assets, including the pensions of Bob Robinson and hundreds of thousands of other innocent people. Emrae International was nearly broke when Sittinz took the Fifth then flew the coop. The employees were in shock and politicians wanted blood.

Now Christmas was over. With his wife, children and four grandkids, Bob Robinson celebrated a blessed Christmas. Without his life savings, the Robinson family needed to enjoy the holiday and lean on each other.

The custodian stood on top of the credenza behind the desk of the CEO holding the heavy garbage can in his hand. His eyes filled with tears as he looked through the huge glass window toward the lights of the city. Robinson took one last look at the Truman Sport Complex to his right, Riss Lake to his left, then down to the ant-sized cars buzzing back and forth on the boulevard below.

How could a person be so greedy and hard-hearted? he wondered. Robinson had been a loyal member of the Emrae International team throughout his career. During his tenure he had humbly served six different chairmen. All were good men and helped Emrae to grow and prosper. When Curtis Sittinz took over, he automatically earned the loyalty of Bob Robinson. The new CEO was full of charisma and always had a smile for the custodian. Why shouldn't he? The two of them were partners in Robinson's pension account.

Dutifully, he invested the maximum he could afford into his pension fund and authorized every penny to be invested in the stock of his beloved company. His August pension statement showed a balance of $205,101.21. Each quarter he would proudly pin his account printout on a corkboard in his bedroom. By the time the holidays arrived, his account had dropped to less than five thousand dollars.

He opened his worn brown wallet and looked once more at the pictures of his wife and grandchildren. He turned back to look at the Chairman's desk. Robinson raised the heavy gold plated wastebasket high over his head and smashed it through the window causing shards of shattered glass to explode out and down toward the street below. He grabbed his vacuum cleaner and hurled it and himself through the window. He lost consciousness and his heart convulsed as he fell past the twenty-first floor. His spirit, embraced by a brilliant white light, was totally oblivious to the sickening thud of his corpse hitting the unforgiving concrete.

CHAPTER TWO

THE WHITE HOUSE OVAL OFFICE
WASHINGTON, D.C.

"Mr. President, Attorney General Austin and Senator Wilder are here to see you."

"Send them in, Jordan," ordered President D.M. Hage. The President of the United States rubbed his eyes and brushed his fingers through his graying temples as he rose from his desk to greet his two guests. One was his long-time confidant and the other his perpetual nemesis.

"Mr. President, nice to see you again," said the United States Senator from Idaho. His words shrouded his little white lie. The President took his hand and gave a half-hearted shake, along with a suspicious smile.

"Mr. President, it's always a pleasure to be with you," said the A.G. as the Commander in Chief gave him a hug and patted his back three times. Austin was shorter than the President and deeply tanned from playing golf. The game was his passion and he played every chance he could. His friendship with President Hage started when the two were college classmates then attended law school together.

"Please take a seat," the President said, with open palms gesturing to the sitting area of the Oval Office. He was a little over six feet tall, handsome and possessed an engaging personality. The trio sat and ordered beverages from the butler. The President had a glass of red wine, the A.G. a diet Pepsi and the Senator a Jack Daniel's on the rocks with a splash of water. Senator Wilder was an avid JD fan but, unfortunately for him, his acquired taste for the beverage had gotten him into trouble a time or two.

The Attorney General and the President had closely supported each other through thick and thin. With Hage elected to the highest office in the land, they were enjoying thick times now. Hage appointed Austin to the highest legal office in the country. Senator Wilder had stridently opposed the nomination but time had healed a good deal of that wound. Anyway, that's how political life worked in the District of Colombia. Today's mortal enemy can be tomorrow's ally.

Wilder had been elected to the Senate from the Great State of Idaho for six terms and had become a fixture in Washington. His hair had turned completely white, his belly bulged and there was a slight stoop in his back. His popularity back home was unchallenged and even though he was from a state that had just over one million people, his prestige and power in the nation's Capital were considerable. Both political parties were well aware of his influence, particularly on issues of national security.

There was no time for small talk. "What's the latest?" demanded the President.

"Prime Minister Louis Phillipe of the Federal Republic of Tropican has made an absolute and final decision that the former CEO of Emrae International, Curtis Sittinz, will now and forever enjoy safe haven," said the Attorney General.

"Shit," exclaimed the President, "the dumb son-of-a-bitch has got to have rocks in his head. Hasn't he figured out after all the secret negotiations we've had with his people that we're gonna bring the wrath of God down on him? We'll hit his ass with sanctions, embargo, and strike at the heart of his fraudulent regime? Hell, we may even invade his corrupt little nirvana!"

"Mr. President, we've threatened, bullied and even tried to blackmail the horny bastard, but he just won't give in. Sittinz has bought him but good and he ain't gonna give him up," said Austin.

"Senator Wilder, you and I have crossed swords in lots of ways through the years. In fact, on most issues I haven't been able to find any support from you with a search warrant. But, on this one, we just have to agree. Don't we?"

"Absolutely, yes, Mr. President. This crook tried to buy all of us, Republicans and Democrats alike, with money he stole from grandmas and grandpas throughout the country."

"Throughout the world," corrected the A.G.

Senator Wilder leaned forward. His belly stretched the bright red suspenders bulging from under his open suit coat. "You're damn right. He had worldwide offices and peddled his poison pension program in forty-nine states. I just thank God he didn't set up shop in Idaho. The rotten scumbag bilked innocent investors out of their hard-earned pensions with his phantom stock scheme then cut and run with their money to his little utopia in Tropican. I'm with you on this, Mr. President. We can't let this lowlife get away with it."

"I appreciate your support. You can really help by keeping your side of the aisle behind our efforts on this one. For us to work with your colleagues solo would be like trying to herd a bunch of rattlesnakes. If Phillipe wants to play hardball, we'll fire a fastball right to the side of the scoundrel's thick skull."

The President stood and walked resolutely behind his desk and pressed the intercom button on his telephone, "Jordan, get me the Chairman of the Joint Chiefs on the phone, scramble line, as quickly as you can."

"Yes, sir."

Wilder drained his glass and signaled for a refill. The butler knew his job well and already had a fresh cocktail on his tray. Wilder's reputation preceded him, even with the President's personal staff.

Thirty-five seconds later, Chairman Leahy was on the line from his office in the Pentagon, "Mr. President, it's a pleasure to talk to you."

"This has nothing to do with pleasure, General. Are you ready to proceed with the Special Ops we discussed regarding Tropican?"

The General was taken aback and the line was silent for several seconds. "Oh, it's come to that. Yes, Mr. President, we are in place and fully prepared."

CHAPTER THREE

THE PRIME MINISTER'S PALACE
THE FEDERAL REPUBLIC OF TROPICAN

Prime Minister Phillipe won his election the old-fashioned way. He bought it. With the help of his friend Curtis Sittinz, he had held office for three years and brutally consolidated his grip on power. The military was solidly behind him. The officers and soldiers of the Tropican Brigade were the highest paid professionals in the country and the people danced to their tune.

The election math worked out to just over one hundred and twenty-seven dollars per vote for the one million votes that made Phillipe the victor. That was small potatoes compared to the billions Sittinz had spirited away to Tropican. Phillipe's fierce loyalty had been bought and paid for with millions of the billions of dollars the former CEO had stolen from unsuspecting clients of Emrae International, Inc. Sittinz was now clipping coupons and collecting his Machiavellian dividends.

Tropican's economy was bad even before Phillipe gained control of the country. The Prime Minister, along with his ruthless security chief Roberto Castille, made things even worse. Housing was bad and social services non-existent. Phillipe was a terrible dictator who had the vision

of a bat at noon. He poured a fortune into his palace and pet projects.
The nation's debt load actually increased with the infusion of money
from Sittinz because much of the funding Prime Minister Phillipe
received from Emrae was used as down payments for his illicit ventures.
He financed the balance on the backs of his own poor people.

The judicial system was arbitrary and corruption ran rampant.
Bribery started at the lowest levels of business as well as government
and extended upward. The bottom of the pyramid was as rotten as the
top. Under the Phillipe regime, many businesses crumbled and investors
avoided the nation like the plague. Even though the plunder entering
Tropican from Emrae International was a closely guarded secret, big
business could sense that the country was heading for instability and
that revolution would surely follow.

The people were beginning to grow restless but the security chief
did his job well and even the slightest opposition was quickly quelled.
Captain Castille and his personal hardcore corps of Gestapo cruelly
moved in on any revolutionary ringleaders and made examples of them.

The Prime Minister and the charlatan sat on the beach as the ocean
waves lapped on the shores of the palace grounds. Sittinz sat barefooted
drinking a concoction of rum, punch, and mango. Phillipe, now in his
mind a world-class political leader, drank expensive French cabernet to
demonstrate his sophistication.

The dancers, who Phillipe had personally selected for the night's
festivities, were stunning. Each wore a native flower in her hair and a
small slit skirt that started below the navel, ended high on the thigh and
clung tight to the gyrating cheeks of her buttocks. The rest was
completely bare. They all had a similar appearance and size. It was as
if they had come out of the same mold, with attractive dark hair and soft
brown skin. Naked breasts bounced to the pounding rhythm of the
music. The bright moon created a silver streak in the ocean that cast a
romantic spell on the revelry.

A red-hot fire puffed cinders into the air and the beat of the drums
intensified. The dancers kicked sand with their bare feet, as their
movements became more rapid and erotic.

"The difference is in their eyes," said Phillipe when his guest
commented on how the beautiful dancers looked so much alike. "Look

closely and select one by looking deeply into her eyes. Are you sure you're man enough to handle a fine female specimen from Tropican? Our women are among the most passionate in the world. They can be very, very hot."

"I think I'll be able to rise to the challenge." Sittinz stood up and stumbled among the dancers while clutching his rum punch as though it was liquid gold. He took another big swig of the concoction and some spilled down his chin. He staggered a little and each time he did so he bumped into a bare breast. He tried to look into their eyes but his gaze kept dropping lower to their shimmering bodies. He finally made his selection and took her by the hand.

"You have selected a fine Tropicanian virgin," said another dancer who was older but every bit as beautiful. "My name is Antoinette. Don't you think you should balance virginity with experience? Take me with you and I will show you the romantic ways of our island." She kissed his bare chest and put her hand inside his shorts. She was persuasive and Sittinz put his arm around her.

The Prime Minister dismissed the rest of the dancers with a wave of his hand. The others weren't departing the palace grounds. They were simply relocating to the Prime Minister's private rookery. Most would spend only one night, however. Then, Captain Castille would personally enlist a new collection of delicacies for the next little beach party.

"Good night, my friend. I look forward to seeing you tomorrow to confer on new opportunities of commerce for my nation. My driver will take you home after you have had time to further discover the beach," teased the Prime Minister with a smirk as he left to investigate his own waiting harem.

Before giving herself up to Sittinz, the virgin dancer tried to exact a promise. "Will you take me back to America with you when you return? My mother has told me to do whatever it takes to escape from Tropican."

"Whatever it takes?" asked the former CEO.

"Yes, anything."

Antoinette echoed the same sentiments and added, "Life here is very difficult for my family. I wish to go to America and earn money so I can help support my brother and sisters."

Sittinz's imagination went wild when both offered *whatever it takes.* He had several whatever's clearly in mind. "Well," he fibbed, "I am the answer to both of your mothers' prayers." Antoinette made no further comment.

Sittinz had absolutely no plans to return to his native country. He had selfishly deserted his wife and two children leaving the three to fend for themselves and face all the shame and condemnation he had created. He would never return. "Of course, I'll take you with me back to America."

The virgin instantly understood that her body was her ticket to a new life. Sittinz rolled over on his side toward the fire as the two island beauties stripped him of his clothes and massaged every inch of his body, every inch. He returned their touches exploring their every mound, crack and crevice. The heat of the moment matched that of the roaring fire. The grinding and copulation on the beach was intense and sweat caused sand to stick to their bodies, which added to the eroticism. When the fornication was complete a totally satisfied but exhausted Sittinz rolled to his back and looked up at the stars.

Antoinette was forced to use her powers of persuasion one more time. It was too early to leave the beach. She had to keep him occupied for another thirty minutes. She handed him the remainder of his drink, which now contained a dissolved white pill she added while he wasn't looking. "So soon? Mona has given you her virginity. We must be sure that it is a memorable night for her. It is the romantic way of the island, you know."

She used her tongue to tantalize her quarry. It worked. Sittinz became aroused once again. Antoinette positioned Mona on top of him and the two had intercourse once again. Mona's toes dug deep into the soft white sand when he came inside her.

The island dancers lay on each side of him with their head and arms on his chest and their legs covering his naked loins, Mona seemed to be dreaming of her new life in America and Antoinette counted the minutes.

I've got it made now, he thought, *more money than I can ever spend, an endless supply of beautiful women and complete safety and protection in paradise. Nobody can touch me now!*

CHAPTER FOUR

THE SKIES ABOVE THE FEDERAL REPUBLIC OF TROPICAN

The unmanned Predator aircraft did not carry a Hellfire missile for this mission. This one was not search and destroy, but search and snatch. This Predator's payload included a video camera sending live pictures to the television monitor the Special Operations Force was eagerly watching in preparation for its upcoming clandestine mission. The Force, orbiting above the predator, was poised and ready to jump into action. Resources and information in country were excellent because the CIA had substantial reconnaissance assets on the ground. There were plenty of friendlies in Tropican, and the American spies working inside the country had more than enough cover and assistance. The Predator had been directed to the exact location where former Emrae International CEO Sittinz was thought to be located.

Eighteen highly trained Navy SEALs, faces darkened, huddled in the belly of the Special Operations Seahawk helicopter hovering over the target. The crew of three normally chauffeured eleven troops. However, for this occasion the seats had been removed to allow a larger complement of Special Forces.

Night vision goggles, mounted on their helmets, were ready to snap in place and instantly light up the darkness. This same elite unit had honed their skills in the rugged mountains of eastern Afghanistan. The commandos had trained for this mission over and over again. It would involve all three of the dimensions that were represented in the creation of the acronym SEAL, Sea-Air-Land.

Each member of the team knew exactly what was expected of him and was willing to give his life to ensure the success of the operation and the safety of his countrymen. Quick action and the element of surprise were their allies. There was complete silence as grim faces watched the monitor displaying the images being sent by the Predator.

An AC-130 gunship was just off the coast to back up the SEALs if necessary.

The Commander sat next to a young handsome black SEAL who appeared to be the most determined among a group of very determined unconventional warriors.

"Robinson, are you ready to go?"

"Yes, sir. Locked and loaded," he said as he kissed the barrel of his weapon. He gritted his teeth and the muscles in his jaw stiffened. The young patriot had looked forward to this night every moment of every day of his life since Christmas.

"I know you've got special emotions on this one, son. We have got to go by the book, though. I don't blame you for wanting to make sure this rogue is brought to justice."

Navy SEAL Robert Robinson Jr. graduated at the top of his class. His athleticism, bravery, and strong work ethic made him stand out in a crowd. As he leaned forward, with his forehead on his weapon barrel, he thought back to his last Christmas. He remembered the wonderful holiday dinner he shared with his family. He recalled putting his arms around his father and thanking him for all he had done to help him succeed in life. His dad had worked hard to provide for his family.

I love you dad, Robinson thought. *I know you're watching from heaven. This is for you.*

"Yes, sir, Commander. I understand what you are saying. I've got my emotions under control. This op will be handled with complete professionalism. You can count on me."

"I know that. Okay men; let's protect each other's back. I want Robinson to lead this mission and you all know why."

"Damn right, Commander," shouted one the SEALs and the others nodded in agreement.

The Predator located the target returning to his mansion after the late night orgy at the Prime Minister's Palace had climaxed. Antoinette had done her job well and the timing was absolutely perfect. The SEAL Commander gave a hand signal to attack and the helicopter swooped in low above the limousine in which Sinnitz was riding.

"Ready, Bob, Jr.?" asked the Commander.

"Ready, Commander. Goggle up. SEAL team, let's roll," screamed Robinson as he waved for his teammates to follow him out the helicopter.

The SEAL team slid down from the sky on ropes and floated over the limo as the long vehicle came to a stop. Sittinz was groggy from the combination of alcohol and the mickey Antoinette had put in his drink. He offered no resistance. Ten seconds after the former CEO's car door opened, he was hooded, handcuffed and hijacked from his tropical hideaway.

SEAL Robinson handled himself in an exemplary manner but when he handcuffed the prisoner he tightened the cuffs with an extra hard squeeze. He could feel Sittinz stiffen with pain and Jr. allowed himself a tiny gratifying smirk as he held his teeth and jaws tightly shut with determination.

Next stop? The U.S. Naval Station at Guantanamo Bay, Cuba. It was an appropriate place to deliver Sittinz. Before the United States occupied the Bay in 1898, during the Spanish-American War, Guantanamo had served as a pirate stronghold in the days of the Spanish Main. Now, a notorious modern-day pirate was soon to land at the closed port on the southeast coast of Cuba.

The Pearl of the Antilles had been the resting-place for Christopher Columbus in 1494 during his second voyage to the New World. However, the iniquitous former CEO would find no comfort or rest in Cuba because his visit would be short-lived.

The pilot in command of the Seahawk had the 3400 horses of the twin turbine General Electric engines flat out. The chopper streaked over the ocean below, toward its destination, in excess of one hundred and sixty knots. "Two minutes to Gitmo," announced the SEAL Commander. "Hunker down."

The prisoner was lying face down on the helicopter's floorboards, completely surrounded by his captors. They leaned against the sides of the aircraft and steadied themselves for landing. They kept their weapons trained on their captive the entire time. Even though Sittinz was now virtually helpless, it was the emotion and satisfaction of the snatch that drove the troops to carefully monitor their hooded convict and make absolutely sure he didn't move a muscle without their permission.

As a courtesy, the State Department had briefed Cuban President Fidel Castro that the Navy was bringing the former Emrae International CEO to the Naval Base located in his country. Relationships between the two countries were mildly warming after more than four decades of bitterness.

There was no need to embarrass the Castro regime by having them learn, after the fact, that Sittinz would be a "tourist" in their land. After all, Castro and his people didn't make a fuss when Guantanamo became the host base for Camp X-ray where terrorist Al Qaeda members and detainees from the fallen Taliban regime in Afghanistan were brought and incarcerated. There was also no outcry when the temporary holding area became a permanent detention center at the base named Camp Delta that housed detainees from over thirty countries.

Plus, the embargo in place by the United States against Cuba was being debated in Congress and the Cubans were buying millions of dollars worth of American agricultural food products. The State Department wanted to be sure no feathers were ruffled and communicated through diplomatic channels. As a precaution, the diplomatic channels were not utilized until *after* Sittinz was securely under the control of the SEALs and had already been whisked out of the airspace of Tropican.

Robinson and his fellow SEALs delivered Sittinz to the base at Guantanamo with clockwork precision. The instant the chopper touched the tarmac, the doors flew open and six SEALs jumped out on both sides of the craft to enforce maximum security. The remaining six yanked the prisoner, still hooded, from the starboard side of the helicopter and dragged him twenty yards across the runway to the port side of a waiting jet.

The plane had been pre-positioned for takeoff at the end of the base's south runway facing into the wind. The plane's Rolls Royce Tay turbofan engines, already running, were generating an enormously high-pitched roar. Four SEALs pulled their captured prey up the main entry doorsteps. The instant they had the criminal, Sittinz, inside the jet and buckled in, the entry door was slammed shut.

Robinson stayed on the ground in Cuba. The Commander wanted the young SEAL to be able to avenge his father's death and knew he would carry out his duties as he had been trained. However, there was no need to tempt fate and have the young SEAL closely confined in the jet for several hours with Sittinz.

Robinson's heart pounded as he watched the jet prepare for takeoff. He reached inside his uniform and took out the picture of his father he had carried in his pocket during the daring mission. Tears welled up in his eyes and he looked up to heaven as he whispered, "We got him. I love you, dad."

CHAPTER FIVE

THE MANSION OF VINCENTE VITORRI
BUFFALO, NEW YORK

The jet-black Lincoln Town Car sped toward its destination at high speed. It raced past two Buffalo police department cruisers, both of which turned to follow but quickly backed off after checking the license plates and realizing who it was.

The Lincoln screeched to a halt in front of the huge iron gates guarding the entrance to the estate of Don Vincente Vitorri. It was two minutes before four in the morning. The driver anxiously hammered the intercom button. The mansion's security cameras blinked on and drowsy guards jumped to life.

"Jesus, Carmine," blurted the senior security guard on duty, "it's four in the morning. What in the hell are you doing here this time of day?"

"Open the gate. I have information that Don Vittori needs to hear immediately," yelled the passenger in the back seat of the Lincoln.

"You know he goes to bed late and likes to get up at the crack of noon. He's not gonna like being disturbed like this."

"Open the gate and open it now! Tell Santino to awaken the Don.

I must speak to him at once," commanded Vitorri's personal attorney Anthony Cordero.

The gates slowly swung open and the car sped up the tree-lined driveway as lights clicked on inside the residence. Even before the Lincoln came to a complete stop, Cordero jumped out of the car and hurried to the imposing front doors of the mansion.

"Don Vittori will be down in a moment," announced the capo Santino as he opened the heavy wooden doors and allowed Cordero to enter. "He will meet you in the library." Santino, unshaven and in white T-shirt and shorts was angered to be awakened so early.

The barrister paced nervously back and forth in the library while he waited for the boss to come down from his master bedroom.

"Why the hell are you on a mission before the sun comes up? This is totally un-Italian," complained the capo.

"Shhh," shushed the consiglio as he put his index finger on his lips. Santino said no more. Cordero was given espresso and some biscotti by the mansion's cook who was awakened by the commotion. Cordero sipped the drink loudly and repeatedly dunked the biscotti in the cup to soften it.

Don Vincente Vittori appeared in the open doorway of the library. He wore a purple bathrobe with matching slippers and had a thick scarf around his neck. The Don was half-awake but alert. "Consiglio, why do you come to me so early in the morning?" asked the old man in a soft voice.

"Sittinz has been kidnapped from Tropican. Phillipe was powerless to stop it. Do you understand? Our partner, the former CEO of Emrae International, is now under the control of the feds! My guess is that he's headed to a federal prison for merciless interrogation about what and who was involved in the Emrae scandal."

"Dear Jesus, how can this happen?" asked Vittori as he walked under a crucifix hanging on the library wall. "Sittinz is a weak sister. He will crack wide open under questioning and finger us in a New York minute. He has the balls of a field mouse. How can we get to him?"

"In federal custody, it is virtually impossible," said the attorney as he sucked the espresso out of the biscotti and continued to pace back and forth across the room.

Don Vincente Vittori was visibly shaken.

"We either get him the best defense team in America to free him from federal custody or somehow silence him," counseled Cordero. "We have no time to waste before we take action. What is your wish?" It was a curious question by the solicitor because he had never discussed the possibility of killing anybody with Vittori. The Don was very careful to isolate knowledge regarding his business practices. He doled out information on a need to know basis to protect himself from any possible traitor within the family.

Vittori closed his eyes and rubbed his forehead as he pondered the question. After a few moments he answered firmly, "Maybe both."

CHAPTER SIX

THE WHITE HOUSE OVAL OFFICE, WASHINGTON, D.C.

"Yes!" screamed President Hage as he pumped his clenched fist high in the air and jerked it down hard as a sign of victory. "Give General Leahy another star and eighteen medals to those brave Navy SEALs who snatched that bastard right from under Phillipe's nose. Yes! Yes! Yes!" He squealed as he punched the air with clenched fist three more times in celebration.

"Yes, sir," cheered the Attorney General. "I couldn't agree more! Maybe you should present the star and medals on national TV. It will draw a huge audience and serve as a defining moment for your Presidency."

"Maybe I will. Damn it, I will," concluded the Commander in Chief as he continued his merriment like a batter who had just hit a grand slam to win the World Series.

"Excellent," declared Austin, "I'll co-ordinate it through your White House spokesman." His jubilation turned to serious conversation. "Mr. President, we must remember we've gotten in bed with the devil to make sure we pulled this off without a hitch."

"I know, we'll have to live up to our part of the bargain but it's the lesser of two evils and we're a hell of a lot better off with the lesser."

"I understand, but we're going to need to keep a tight lid on the details, including our new friend."

"Mr. President, Senator Wilder is here as you requested," announced Jordan.

"Send him right in," ordered Hage. "No talk about our secret arrangement in front of Wilder. You hear me?"

"Yes, of course, I won't say a word."

The lock to the door of the Oval Office snapped open and Senator Carl Wilder entered.

"Mr. President, congratulations on a magnificent attack and snatch. Your courageous action has won the hearts and minds of a worried nation."

"Senator Wilder, you've dogged my ass for twenty years. But tonight, let's just celebrate our achievement."

"Doggoned right. Let's have a hot damn party. Pour me the Pride of Lynchburg in a bucket of ice and I'll toast you to high heaven. Hell, I'll sleep in the Lincoln Bedroom and even make a whole one dollar donation to your re-election campaign."

"Done," said the President.

Senator Wilder awoke the next morning with a pounding headache. He sat up in a hard strange bed and focused on a picture of a fuzzy bearded man with a big nose. Wilder rubbed his eyes and into clear view came none other than Abraham Lincoln himself. It was a portrait of the sixteenth President of the United States. The Senator's thoughts turned to the Gettysburg Address, the Civil War, and Ford's Theater as he gazed at the historic portrait hanging on the wall.

Now he remembered the celebration of the capture of Sittinz, the toasts and even the crisp one-dollar bill he had given to the re-election fund for President Hage. Though they were from opposing political parties, it was critical for Senator Wilder to support Hage in the Emrae International scandal. Getting to the bottom of the affair and dispensing justice crossed party lines.

The White House butler was on the spot the minute Senator Wilder sat up in bed. On his tray he offered coffee, orange juice and aspirin just in case. The Senator chose orange juice to wash down three aspirin tablets.

He showered, soaped and even sang a couple of off-tune songs while washing off the lather. He dried and dressed in preparation for the morning's press conference on the south lawn of the White House where he, representing the loyal opposition, would demonstrate bipartisan support for the President's bold action.

CHAPTER SEVEN

ONBOARD THE YACHT *TABOO*
FORTY NAUTICAL MILES OFF THE COAST OF NEW YORK

Taboo was a splendid ship, which sailed under Bahamian registry. Her one hundred and seventy-five-foot hull was built in the Benetti Shipyard in Viareggio, Italy where Europe's finest craftsmen finished her. Boat building began in the seaside resort at the dawn of the 19th century. Since that time many of the world's finest yachts have slid down the ways in Viareggio, making Italy one of the most prolific boat-building countries in the world. In 1873 Lorenzo Benetti opened his own shipyard in the village. This was the world-renowned shipyard that had built *Taboo*.

The megayacht's broad beam created exceptional roominess inside *Taboo*. Her four decks were opulent in every way and had been carefully designed to give *Taboo* a sleek, modern look. The top deck contained the Captain's quarters which were just a few steps from the yacht's bridge. A large helipad was located at the stern of the upper deck. This is where Emrae International's now deposed CFO Andrew Bronson would soon be landing.

Vincente Vittori sat in the living area of his personal quarters located amidships on the main deck. It was a comfortable private space lined with walnut-colored African wood. With him were his legal counsel Anthony Cordero and, of course, his omnipresent bodyguard Santino. Vittori wore black slacks and a heavy dark plum sweater that contrasted with his gray hair. He sat in an oversized brown leather chair with his feet propped up on an ottoman. "Antonio, what in hell happened to Prime Minister Phillipe's promise that nobody could touch Sittinz while he was under his protection in Tropican?"

"We're looking into it, but he's no match for U.S. military forces. Who would have thought Hage would have had the guts to violate Tropican's sovereignty and snatch him right off the island? He's taking some heat from the United Nations but he doesn't seem to give a damn about that."

"I don't give a damn about that either. The only thing I give a damn about is protecting us from being exposed."

"I understand. It still astounds me Hage was able to have his people pull off such a feat. If Tropican soldiers had been around and shot down that helicopter or killed some of the SEALS the President would have had a major political disaster on his hands. I guess he just got lucky."

"Maybe so, but it was bad luck for us. Tell me more about this Andrew Bronson," said Vittori with the wave of his hand.

"He was the Chief Financial Officer of Emrae for the last four years and Sittinz's right-hand man. Sittinz didn't take a shit without Bronson handling the paperwork. He knows every detail of our relationship with Emrae. He assures me we can count on his complete loyalty. To prove it, he's invoked the Fifth Amendment three times already and hasn't uttered a peep to the FBI or press, yet."

"Yet," cautioned Vittori.

"He is coming here at your request, Don Vittori and he's helped us make a pile of money," said the attorney. "He can still be very useful as we finalize the details of our arrangement with Sittinz."

"We'll see," said the Don.

The conversation was interrupted by the flutter of helicopter blades as a chopper closed in on the helipad above them. The aircraft's skids gently touched the surface of the ship and settled in as the engine shut down and the big blades slowed. Santino, head ducked down, ran to the door of the helicopter and opened it. He grabbed Bronson's arm and led him to Vittori's suite but said nothing. When they reached the bottom of the spiral staircase leading from the upper deck, Santino opened the door to admit Bronson into the Don's presence.

"Welcome Andy," said the attorney with his hand extended. "Let me introduce you to Mr. Vincente Vittore."

"Mr. Vittore, I am honored to meet you," offered the nervous bean counter as he bowed his head in respect.

"As I am to meet you," said Vittori. "Please, have a seat so we can get to know each other. We have a great deal to talk about."

The yacht's chief steward entered the owner's private quarters with crystal wine goblets and a bottle of heavy red wine that had previously been decanted and allowed to breathe. He placed plates of antipasto in front of each man and poured the wine. The steward then respectfully backed out of the room to allow privacy.

Vincente Vittori was not one to mince words. "Our organization is not about to be brought into the Emrae International fiasco. We will do whatever is necessary to eliminate any possible attempt to pull us in. Do you understand what I am talking about, Mr. Bronson?"

"Mr. Vittori, I absolutely do. I have not uttered a word about your involvement and I never will. You can count on that."

"Who else knows of our participation in this–this situation?" Vitorri demanded. "Other than you and Curtis Sittinz, who else?"

"Nobody. We kept our relationship totally secret from the Board of Directors of Emrae and all other executives," insisted Bronson.

"What about your assistants or others in the firm who could have accidentally read documents, signed wire transfers or figured out any possible connection?" pressed the Don.

Bronson tugged on his ear as he thought. "The only remotely possible person is my own accounting assistant, Michael Sanderson, but I seriously doubt he has any idea because we have never discussed it and he has never once mentioned it. Even if he did, it would be pure speculation at best. I will never say a word, even if they hang me from the yardarm."

Vittori was convinced and the discussion ended. Bronson was excused to go to his stateroom to freshen up and dress for dinner. His small suitcase had already been delivered to his room. His clothes and personal items had been unpacked for him and a fresh shirt pressed and hung in the closet. It was a courteous gesture by the crew but one which also allowed for close inspection of everything Bronson had brought on board with him. Cordero also left Vittori's private quarters to dress for dinner but Santino stayed behind to privately confer with the Don for a few more minutes.

Thirty minutes later the group reconvened in the luxurious dining room located aft on the third deck of *Taboo*. Santino did not attend the dinner, but the three, the Don, the defender and the deposed, started the evening with stiff cocktails. Dinner included salad, pastas, veal scaloppini, polenta and baked breads complemented with virgin olive oil. Chianti and two drier red wines, one French and one Italian, were poured in copious quantity. By the time tiramisu and after-dinner drinks were presented, Bronson was loaded and dog-tired.

"Bridge," stiffly answered the captain, himself, who was at the helm of the grand yacht.

"This is Santino. Continue playing music from the Italian Opera Madame Butterfly through the speakers on the third deck dining room. Mr. Vittori enjoys that music while he dines."

"Yes, of course, sir."

"Pipe the soundtrack from the movie *Titanic* through the rest of the yacht and turn the volume up high."

"*Titanic?*" shrieked the captain over the intercom. "Forgive me, but *Titanic* is not the favorite of seafaring men."

"Do as you are instructed and turn the volume up," ordered the Sicilian as he slammed the phone handset into its cradle to add an exclamation point to his command.

Santino was very intimidating and the captain did as he was told. The first mate hopped to and placed the compact disc of the sound track into the audio player and cranked the volume up.

"I wondered why he brought this soundtrack on board. It is not the best selection for an ocean journey," complained the second-in-command.

"Never mind, first mate. Now go down to the galley and muster the rest of the crew there with you and stay there until you hear from me. Chef Ellen has prepared a fine meal. Now that dessert has been served,

Mr. Vittori wants to be left alone to speak with his guest before he departs by helicopter."

"But, captain?"

The yacht commander interrupted him in mid-sentence. "Do as you are told. Remember, when I first hired you I told you that the crew of a fine yacht is deaf and dumb. Nothing you see or hear on such a vessel is ever repeated. Do you remember?"

"Yes, sir."

The captain stayed in the wheelhouse looking straight ahead as Mr. Vittori himself had instructed, while the rest of the crew was sequestered in the galley.

Vittori and Cordero continued to drink and tap their toes to the lively Italian aria while Bronson returned to his stateroom woozy and tired. He scuffed to his door and opened it ready to fall in bed. Santino was waiting inside the darkened stateroom and when the door closed he struck. The Sicilian snapped a three-foot-long rope around Bronson's thin, wrinkled neck and plunged his knee into the small of his victim's back to gain more leverage. Bronson was unable to put up much fight and was left to gag and gurgle as life drained from his body. His eyes nearly popped out and the veins on his neck bulged with a deep sickening blue color. He coughed a gasping cough. The assassin squeezed the rope tighter and tighter as the music from *Titanic* reached a crescendo.

Santino loved his job. Engineering death was his lifework. The bawdy premeditation and execution of murder was an aphrodisiac for him. His twisted mind allowed him to come up with any number of lecherous, kinky schemes he used to execute people. He'd killed with guns but that was so impersonal. He much preferred methods like strangulation and the knife so he could use his fingers and hands up close and personal. The more exotic the kill the more erotic it was to the demented Sicilian. He loved all the minutiae.

Tonight he had perfected his art form to yet another level by even selecting the music to play during the liquidation of Bronson. The loud songs ensured that the crew could not hear any sounds of the crime and as a further precaution he had the helicopter pilot warming up his thunderous turbine engine to create even more noise.

Vittori and Cordero were still drinking and tapping as they remained cocooned in the dining room. The music of *Titanic* blared over the rest of the speakers of *Taboo* and serenaded the ocean waves as the magnificent yacht drifted in the calm sea.

The vile act of murder stirred Santino's carnal desires. He actually had an orgasm when Bronson's lifeless body went limp. "Aaaaahh," he sighed as the sick passion of the moment came to a climax. He let loose of the rope for an instant, then gave it one more violent jerk to make sure he had completed the job.

Santino let the body fall to the floor, took his cell phone from his pocket and called the pilot waiting on the helipad. The rope was still wrapped around his left hand as he held the phone to his ear.

"Yo," answered the pilot.

"Go ahead and take off. Your passenger has decided to spend the night on the yacht and will return to the mainland tomorrow."

"Remember, I told you I was tied up on company business tomorrow and I could only borrow this chopper for tonight."

"Yes, I will have another pilot from a different company take care of our guest in the morning," said the Sicilian. "I've placed an envelope on your co-pilot seat to take care of your expenses."

The pilot opened the envelope, "Oh, very generous. Thank you." With that the chopper quickly lifted off the helipad. All the moonlighting pilot knew was that he had delivered an unnamed guest to the yacht and somebody else would return him to the mainland tomorrow.

"Well, Mr. Vittori's guest is off to the wild black yonder," observed the first mate as he and the others continued eating in Chef Ellen's galley. The assassin, Santino, had created the illusion of a common shell game. The pilot believed the guest was spending the night on the yacht and the crew knew he had left the yacht because they saw him fly away on the helicopter. It was a perfect cover.

Santino put the corpse in a body bag and dragged it with all of Bronson's clothing and personal items to the stern of the yacht. He unzipped the body bag and added weights then opened his switchblade and made six cuts about a foot long each. The holes in the bag would allow easy access by creepy-crawler bottom feeders, squid, eel and sea pig. Santino made especially sure the holes were big enough to allow the big sharp-toothed mouths of rattail fish, a common sight around the remains of the *Titanic*, to enter the bag, feast away on the accountant's corpse and digest all the evidence.

The killer opened the yacht's swim platform and pushed the coffin into the ocean. Bubbles rose from the bag and dissipated at the surface in a macabre rhythm seemingly choreographed to the music of *Titanic*.

Santino took the small suitcase and contents to the onboard incinerator and cremated all evidence that Bronson had ever been aboard the yacht.

Nobody would ever know that the CFO had been whacked. He would be just like Sittenz, who had run. Only, in Andrew Bronson's case, he would never be found.

CHAPTER EIGHT

THE RHODE ISLAND ROOM
RENAISSANCE MAYFLOWER HOTEL
WASHINGTON, D.C.

President Hage chose the Rhode Island Room in the Mayflower Hotel for the meeting because of its proximity to the White House. The adjoining South Carolina and Pennsylvania Rooms were buffers occupied by the Secret Service. The historic hotel was a perfect place to discuss a history-making decision regarding Emrae International and former CEO Sittinz. Attorney General Austin, two of his lieutenants, and Senator Wilder joined the President for the breakfast conference.

Orange juice, steaming pots of coffee, fruit plates, muffins, Raisin Bran cereal, and two-percent milk were all on the table in advance of the group's arrival so there would be no interruptions from the Mayflower staff.

"Any word on the whereabouts of Andrew Bronson?" asked the President.

"Nothing," said the A.G., "it's as though he disappeared from the face of the earth."

"Well, it's only been a few days since he flew the coop like Sittinz. The world's not big enough for him to hide too long. We'll find his ass

and bring him back just like Sittinz." He looked at the A.G. "Okay,
General Austin, what do we do with Sittinz now? I want to move fast.
We need to try and save what's left of people's pensions just as quickly
as possible. Then we'll give Sittinz his right of due process. He gets a
fair trial and then we put him in a federal penitentiary for the rest of his
rotten life."

"The defense is going to want a change of venue out of Federal
Court. They'll say he can't get a fair trial anywhere in America,"
declared Austin. "They won't win in the end, but they could delay the
proceedings for months while what's left of many pensions will be
going down the drain."

"How the hell do we get cracking on this?" asked the President. "I
don't want to leave any room for this vermin to plea bargain and wiggle
his way out of this thing. Let's be darn sure, too, there is no chance for
some snake oil mistrial."

"Austin told me about this little problem last night and I've got a
thought that just might work," offered Senator Wilder.

"Go on."

"Mr. President, the war on terrorism is resulting in some good things
along with some bad. Tribunal trials by the military are now possible.
Tribunals give lots more latitude to reach verdicts and apply punishments
than normal criminal proceedings. The E.I. mess theoretically qualifies
for tribunal status 'cause it's international in scope, includes economic
terrorism and goes way beyond any plain ol' ordinary crime. The
defense wants to get the proceedings out of the big metropolitan areas
where so many victims of the Emrae debacle live. They'd also jump at
the chance to hold the trial in what they would consider some small-
town Mayberry RFD Courthouse as opposed to an almighty Federal
Court. There is literally only one state in the Union that did not have an
Emrae International presence and that is my home state of Idaho."

"How come Emrae didn't have production offices in Idaho?" asked
Austin's junior aide.

"To be honest with you, although I'd deny I said it, we tried to get
them to come to our state. You know jobs, the economy and all. But,
since the dung hit the fan, we're damn glad they didn't come. Some of
the people investigating this mess have told me the reason they didn't

invade our terrain is because of our good ol' State Constitution. There's a section in Article XI, I think its section nine, or nineteen that talks about fictitious corporate stock increases and indebtedness and that language evidently scared the hell out of 'em. I think the language was probably put in way back when we left territorial status and became the 43rd state in 1890. For that matter, the so-called stock the framers were talking about might have even been stock like cattle. Who knows? Anyway, the Emrae bigwigs thought it was a modern-day trap we could snare 'em in. They figured there was a big possibility that if Idaho invoked that article, it'd blow their whole operation sky high. I guess we weren't worth the risk. Of course, we're gonna take some major credit for being a hell of a lot smarter than the other forty-nine states! You know, our forefathers were sharper than everybody else's forefathers were. Lewis and Clark picked Idaho for their little journey cause we were so brilliant and stuff like that."

"You mean to tell me nobody in your state lost any money on Emrae International?" asked the aide.

"Sure, some of our citizens invested in E.I. stock and lost money and that's bad. But, it's not nearly as bad as losing everything in retirement nest eggs. Section ten in that same Article of our Constitution says we won't recognize a business incorporated out of state or country unless they have at least one place of business within our borders. They were scared to register with our Secretary of State 'cause of the fictitious stock language, so their putrid pension programs weren't allowed to grow without triggering our state income taxes. Consequently, they weren't able to sell their pension scheme to our Idaho citizens. Hell, now that I think of it, I believe we did have superior forefathers."

Wilder continued to explain the strategy he was suggesting to the President. "I'd sell the defense on moving the proceedings to Idaho in exchange for letting ordinary citizens exercise some of that tribunal power."

"Senator, why in the world do you think the defense would go for that?" asked the skeptical Attorney General.

"Because we can sell 'em on the idea that we Idahoans are a bunch of rednecks who don't have any use for big government. They'll think they can win there," said Wilder.

"Well, will they?" asked one of the A.G. aides. "You got a reputation out there. You know, freedom fighters, bigots and all."

"Bullshit," shot back the Senator. "We got lots of great people and fewer bigots in the whole state than live in one block in D.C. A few years back we had some bigot seeds blow in on the wind from California. They imbedded themselves in our soil for a little while but they didn't take root. Remember that it was a Coeur d'Alene, Idaho, jury that poured $6.3 million worth of Roundup on those weeds and burned their ass. It was so hot they jumped back up into the wind and flew to Ohio or Pennsylvania or someplace. Most of 'em are outta Idaho now, that's for sure. Idaho folks will burn Sittinz's ass, Mr. President. You can count on that."

"Hmmm," mouthed the President as he rubbed his chin with his thumb and index finger, pondering the intriguing possibilities of the Senator's thought.

"Mr. President you do have the tribunal powers that were enacted at the start of the war on terrorism. However, there could be some backlash if you try to use them on a non-terrorism case," cautioned Austin's senior aide.

"You know son," scolded Senator Wilder, "you are probably one smart dude when it comes to being a legal scholar with your Ivy League degree and all, but you need to come out west and grow a set of balls."

The aide stood in anger and Austin quickly put his hand on the aide's shoulder and pushed him back down in his chair.

"I've already given the President my word that I'll keep the troops on my side of the aisle in line on this one so politics are not gonna come into play," assured the Senator. "Your party appointed six of the judges sitting on the highest court in the land and this President himself appointed half of those. Most of 'em aren't much good but at least they know where their bread's buttered. This is one time where both sides of the legislative branch will combine with the judicial folks to fully support the executive branch. There ain't gonna be any backlash when it comes to everyone agreeing on a tribunal process. I'm convinced even the defense jackasses will agree to the deal. If the President signs the order it will be carried out, period."

"You have obviously given this a great deal of consideration,

Senator," responded President Hage. "You sound very confident that an Idaho jury will mete out justice. Will it be the kind of justice you and I want?"

"Damn right, I have, and Idahoans will. Attorney General Austin, you've been to Idaho. In fact you've been to Coeur d'Alene, so you know what good people live there. President Hage you should visit Idaho. Hell, go play the floating golf green. The rest of us have to take a boat to that famous fourteenth hole but you can probably just walk out to it. You're a golf fanatic. Plus, they have an army of caddies and some of them are good-lookin' women. You got a little reputation for likin' that," jabbed the Senator.

"Wilder, I thought we made peace for awhile," said Hage.

"We have. I'm supportin' you on this E.I. scandal all the way. Don't get all shook up, I'm just havin' a little fun with you."

Discussions continued for several more hours. Broad concepts were boiled down to finer details. Senator Wilder's idea gradually gained the support of Austin's aides. Everyone wanted to move fast to make the scandal history. After all, the first and most important job any politician has after being elected is to get re-elected. Even though Hage held the highest elected office in the land he was still a politician. The debate was over.

"Attorney General Austin," ordered the President, "You and your boys get the i's dotted and t's crossed on this deal. Move the jurisdiction to Idaho and let's administer justice. I want the Tribunal Orders prepared for my signature and on my desk post haste. I want this trial to be over by next Christmas, if at all possible. We need to get this scandal as far removed from my next Election Day as possible."

The die was cast.

CHAPTER NINE

THE COEUR d'ALENE RESORT
COEUR d'ALENE, IDAHO

Jack Bradley, President of Resort Associates which owned the Coeur d'Alene Resort, called the company's quarterly board meeting to order.

"Christine, will you please call the roll?" asked Bradley.

"Yes, sir. Earl and Betty Hanson?"

"Here."

"Clint Diamond."

"Here," said the handsome movie star who sat at the end of the conference table opposite Bradley.

"Veronica Whitcomb."

"Of course, I'm here. You couldn't possibly have this silly meeting without me," she announced. The wealthy heiress wore a red St. John knit dress that accentuated her beauty. She sat back in her brown leather boardroom chair with her long shapely legs crossed and exposed high on the thighs.

Looking down at the speaker phone on the table, Christine asked, "Senator Wilder are you on the speaker phone from your office in

Washington, D.C.?"

"Yes, Christine I'm on the line. Greetings, partners," said the Senator. "How's life at the top of the world in your fancy condo, Earl and Betty?"

Earl and Betty Hanson lived in Chicago until they won the Illinois State Lottery. They vacationed at the Coeur d'Alene Resort to celebrate their newfound wealth and fell in love with the place. Lady Luck smiled on the Hanson's again when fate brought them together with their adopted daughter, Helen. The Hansons made a decision on that trip to raise her in the lake city and purchased a penthouse in the new McEuen Terrace Condominium Tower downtown.

"Oh, it's just peachy," answered Betty. "The view is to die for. We look at Tubbs hill, the Resort and beautiful Lake Coeur d'Alene." Betty didn't have to sugarcoat her description. She and Earl had found heaven.

"Veronica, I understand you've got some new digs, too," baited the Senator.

"Oh, I do. They are simply marvelous and right on the water. With my splendid interior decorating abilities, I've really made the place quite perfect." Whitcomb was well-heeled. When her tycoon father and mother died she inherited a fortune which allowed her to live an extravagant lifestyle. "However, I do return to my apartment in New York on a regular basis. You know, Senator, my friends in the East deserve to see me once in a while, too."

The Senator raised his eyebrows as if to say, there she goes again. Of course, nobody could see him and he let Veronica's boast go without further comment. She was an oxymoron to him: completely insufferable, yet quite charming.

"We're working on that movie about our heroic Jack Bradley," chimed in movie star Clint Diamond. He was a box office giant who had discovered Coeur d'Alene when he came to play its famous floating green golf course. Jack had been instrumental in preventing the sale of a vital nuclear secret to foreign powers by a traitor who had set up shop in the Resort and Diamond was alluding to that incident.

"Seriously?" asked the Senator.

"Yes, seriously," said the movie star. "Veronica here is putting in some seed money but we're getting lots of interest from the big boys. We'll see."

Jack Bradley was a little shy about the whole thing and broke into the conversation. "Okay, everyone we need to get to work now."

With that, the small talk ended. Jack presented the quarterly financial results. Business was good and no questions were asked but little Helen kept things lively by knocking over a pitcher of water and throwing her dolls on the floor.

"If there is no further business we will now tour the new Whitcomb suite. Veronica has personally handled the remodel and I think you will all be pleased with the wonderful job she did," said Bradley.

"Oh, you are so nice, Jack," sighed Veronica with an unusual hint of humility. "Of course, he's perfectly right. I think all of you will be pleased. At least, I hope so."

"Jack, while the others tour can you stay on the line with me for a moment?" Senator Wilder asked.

"Sure," said Jack, "just give me a minute." He put the phone on hold so he could say goodbye to the directors. Veronica was already waving her hands and explaining how she had brilliantly transformed the suite into a dreamland. Jack picked up the phone. "What's up?"

"I think we may have an opportunity for a little business," whispered Wilder. "The Emrae International scandal is on President Hage's front burner. I just left a meeting where the possibility of a special trial in Coeur d'Alene was discussed."

"You're kidding," replied Jack. "Why would they bring it to Coeur d'Alene?"

"It's a complicated story. I had a little to do with the decision. You know I'm always looking out for what's good for Idaho. The fact that it'll send some business to our hotel won't hurt either. I'll fill you in when I come out next time. Okay?"

"Okay Senator. I'll have the Jack Daniel's on ice when you get here."

"Just make sure you've got a good in with the county bailiff. There's gonna be a sequestered jury and lots of legal beagles in town soon. It'll hit the papers in a day or two."

Chapter Ten

San Francisco, California

Michael Sanderson had served as Andrew Bronson's right-hand man until Bronson, the former CFO of Emrae International, went into hiding. Sanderson wasn't a conspirator in the E.I. scheme and, in fact, had come forward to help expose the fraud. However, because he was considered part of the inner circle, he was advised to seek outside legal advice. He was in San Francisco to consult with the law firm of Hobbins, Davies and Specter where his brother-in-law worked.

Sanderson met with Hobbins and Specter in their office library. His brother-in-law had arranged the meeting but didn't attend due to a conflict in his schedule.

"Why do you think the prosecuting attorneys felt you should have private counsel?" asked Hobbins.

"I'm not sure. I told them everything I know and I think they believed me when I told them I had nothing to do with the scheme our Chairman and CFO were involved in."

Specter opened a book on the table in front of him. He put on his reading glasses and checked the index of the book. "They can't hang you out to dry forever," said Specter. Both attorneys were fairly young but well-trained in their profession. Following graduation from the Gonzaga University School of Law they joined two competing law firms in the Bay Area. After paying their dues with three years of long hours filled with hard, grinding work they decided to go out on their own and invited a former Spokane classmate to join them. "What are you looking for, Jim?" asked Hobbins of his partner.

"I'm trying to find the article and section that defines how long the prosecution has to either charge our client or cut bait."

"Don't worry about that, partner. I have already talked about that with our friend in the prosecutor's office. Remember he is a Bulldog too," said Hobbins, referring to the Gonzaga mascot in which they all took great pride.

"Why didn't you say so in the first place?" said Specter as he closed the book.

"They believe you, Mr. Sanderson. They simply plan to call you to the witness stand to tell everything you do know about the financial practices of the company, accounting procedures and the like. To be honest, you don't really need us but we'll be there for you, if you do."

"You've made my day. In fact you've made my year," said Sanderson.

"My friend in the prosecutor's office asked me to ask one favor of you."

"What's that?"

"If you hear from Andrew Bronson, please let them know right away," advised Hobbins.

"I've already promised them I would. I just can't figure it. Bronson was my boss but I thought of him as a friend, too. It's so unlike him to take off and run like that without a word to anyone. Then again, I never thought he was capable of the terrible things he's evidently been involved in with Sittinz. I just can't believe he can hide forever, no matter how much money he embezzled."

"The FBI and every other spy agency in the world are hunting for him. It's just a matter of time for Bronson," concluded Hobbins. "You, my friend, are in good shape. The only way you can get in trouble now is if you cover for Bronson, if and when he makes contact."

"Understood, and thank you both. Tell my brother-in-law I'll see him in a little bit."

Michael Sanderson felt better than he had since the E.I. scandal broke. He left the attorneys' offices and whistled as he walked out of the high-rise office building.

The attorney's offices were on Pine Street. He wanted some fresh air and decided to walk back on Powell Street to the St. Francis Hotel where he was staying. He and his brother-in-law were going to have a drink together in the hotel's upscale bar, Compass Rose.

At the corner of Post and Powell, he saw a long-haired ruffian grab a handbag from an old lady and run toward Union Square.

Sanderson was an Eagle Scout in his youth where he had learned the slogan, "Do a good turn daily." Instinctively, he raced after the thief who bolted into the underground parking garage and disappeared. As Sanderson sprinted around the corner, a foot stretched out and tripped him. He went flying head over heals and crashed into the concrete wall of the garage. Sanderson was dazed and looked back toward the crook that had tripped him. It wasn't the young thief, but a much older man who was now rushing toward him.

"Oh, I'm so sorry, it was an accident. Are you okay? Let me help you up." As Sanderson stretched out his hand, the blade of an eight-inch knife plunged deep into his heart.

"What . . . why?" were his last words as blood gushed from his chest onto the garage floor.

Santino's face was six inches from his victim's lips and he could hear the last breath come out of Sanderson. He was aroused and twisted the knife blade to create maximum damage. The killer enjoyed the sickening wet squishy sound of tissue and organ being ripped apart.

He pulled his knife from the corpse, wiped the blood off on Sanderson's shirt, then closed the switchblade and put it in his coat pocket. He made sure the accountant was dead by placing his index finger on Sanderson's neck. No pulse, the heart had stopped beating. Santino hurried out of the garage without looking back.

The thug, who snatched the purse for the hundred bucks Santino had slipped him, had no idea he was leading a man to his death. Within hours, the San Francisco police captured the young hoodlum and charged him with first-degree murder. No matter how loud he protested, the police were confident they had arrested the right man.

Santino was in the clear.

CHAPTER ELEVEN

BUFFALO, NEW YORK, & KANSAS CITY, MISSOURI

The rise of Curtis Sittinz in Emrae International had been incredible. When the Board of Directors elected him CEO, the announcement stunned the financial world. He had come out of nowhere to take the helm of one of the nation's largest companies.

The board declared that Sittinz was a brilliant financial strategist who would lead them to the next level. However, no member of the board ever described what the next level was. The seeds of success for Curtis Sittinz had been watered with the blood of his Old World family's violent past.

In the spring of 1923, a spectacular wedding was celebrated at Santa Chiara Catholic Church in Naples, Italy. This was a marriage made in heaven and joined the groom Gisepe Citinzano of the powerful Citinzano family of Milan to the bride Maria Vittori of an equally powerful family from Naples. The Citinzano family's expertise was in the area of law and order as well as in the insurance field. They controlled hundreds of police officials and dozens of judges in northern Italy. When someone needed to have authorities look the other way or persuade a judge to make a particular decision, the advice of the Citinzano Family was sought. They also used their persuasive techniques to extort protection money from various shopkeepers that simply wanted to be left alone and were willing to pay for such insurance.

The Vittori family members were financiers who specialized in banking. Their banks were not the kind where a customer would walk into a tall building with a big vault and speak to a teller. The Vittori branches were located on the sidewalks and back alleys of southern Italy. They provided financing to people who didn't want to declare all of their collateral to banking authorities and were willing to pay a little extra for the anonymity of truly private banking. The Vittori organization serviced clients from Naples south to the toe of Italy's boot.

Both families were very wealthy and had gained reputations for power and ruthlessness. The wedding was one of the grandest Italy had ever experienced. The Italian Catholic Cardinal personally offered a toast to the new couple and even expressed the good wishes of the Pope.

The newlywed couple's first child was a boy and cause for great celebration. However, as the boy grew into a young man he wanted nothing to do with the family business. He had served as an altar boy and almost became a priest so he could work for the good of mankind and Mother Earth. However, as his hormones developed, he realized he was not cut out for celibacy. He also realized he would never escape his family's legacy in the old country and on his twenty-first birthday set sail for America and a new life.

Upon reaching Ellis Island, he assumed the name Sittinz so he would never be identified with the Citinzano label again. His mother secretly sent money every month and the Sittinz family prospered in America. On his deathbed, the elder Sittinz shared the truth with his grandson, Curtis. He had always felt he did the right thing by leaving his family's sinful ways in Italy but also felt a tinge of betrayal. He wanted to purify himself from that tinge before taking his final journey.

Young Curtis had been partially cleansed from the stigma of his family tree by earning an MBA from prestigious Stanford University in Palo Alto, California. He was smart and had earned his degree but took every short cut possible. It was tough to cheat at Stanford but he excelled in even this most difficult of endeavors. He was even able to get an advance copy of the final examination for his course in Business Ethics 101 and aced the class.

His grandfather's deathbed confession tweaked his interest in his familial history when he realized he had larceny in his blood. With the help of a private investigator, he determined that his great-uncle, younger brother of his great-grandfather, who was the patriarch of the family Mafioso, now lived in America, too. His investigative team uncovered the fact that his great-uncle lived in Buffalo, New York, and that his name was Vincente Vittori.

Sittinz persisted, and after months of trying, was finally granted an audience with the elder Vittori. There was an instant bonding and the old and new family blood blended together in a remarkable and distinctively evil way.

"I remember the wedding. I was only six or seven years old but I remember it as though it was yesterday. It was wonderful. It was magical," mused the old man. "My older sister was a beautiful bride and your great-grandfather a handsome young groom. I remember dancing with my mother and my cousins. It was the first time I was allowed to drink a little wine and I even had a taste of fine champagne during one of the toasts."

It was at this first meeting that Don Vincente Vittori, a man with no offspring, realized that the heir to his throne could very well be his long-lost grand-nephew.

Curtis Sittinz left his job as a junior partner in the successful Wall Street brokerage firm of Blythe and Peters and immediately became president of one of his great-uncle's illicit financial enterprises. There was so much money that needed to be laundered in the Vittori Empire that Sittinz couldn't help but become a boy wonder. After all, he didn't have to create the revenue stream. All he had to do was accept the funds and report them as perfectly legitimate profits. He did everything legal to reduce taxes just like any other successful business, but even so there were still enormous profits. Sittinz's firm paid the tax owed to the government just like any other patriotic American company. The laundered money was perfectly clean and ready to be invested. Sittinz was a savvy investor and quickly became a rising star.

Just a few years after their first meeting, Vittori and his protege were faced with an amazing opportunity named Emrae International. Sittinz had been buying stock in the undervalued company and gained such a significant stake that the company's cumulative voting rights allowed him a seat of the Board of Directors. Within a year, the long-time Chairman of Emrae International, who had done an outstanding job in growing the corporation, surprisingly announced his intention to retire. Sittinz sensed this was the time to strike. He needed just three votes, in addition to his own, to take control of the highly profitable company. He was sure he had two votes tied up. Winning the election, by hook or by crook, would put him in a position to fully pillage Emrae's substantial treasury for the benefit of his great-uncle and himself.

The outgoing CEO announced that, even though he would remain on the board, he would not vote on his replacement so there would be no real or perceived conflict of interest. He was respected by the other board members and his wishes were accepted.

"We are in a unique position," Sittinz told Vittori. He explained the possibilities of illegal plunder that would be available if he could successfully win the election and laid out his ingenious plan to begin the larceny immediately upon his inauguration to high office. Sittinz informed his aged relative that the current vote was three to three and the board was hopelessly deadlocked.

"When is the next vote?" the old man asked.

"At our next board meeting in three weeks."

"Get me Santino," ordered the Don as he pulled out a pencil and paper. "Now, who are the three that oppose you?"

One week later a tragic incident left only five members of the board available to vote. The director who most opposed Sittinz had an unfortunate and freak accident. He had taken a terrible fall as he stepped into his bathtub. He slipped on a bar of soap, which had mistakenly been left on the marble floor surrounding the tub and fell headfirst into the faucet of the tub. He died instantly and his body was discovered floating in a pool of blood-red bath water.

The entire Board of Directors attended the funeral. Sittinz read a moving psalm from the Bible and heralded the fallen director's accomplishments in life along with his many valuable contributions to the success of Emrae International. He praised him as the most distinguished director of the company and had a tear in his eye as he proclaimed how much he would be missed. During the reception following the funeral, at the insistence of director Curtis Sittinz, the board agreed their next meeting should be held as scheduled but that a moment of silence should be observed throughout all seventy-two floors of the company's skyscraper where the Board meeting would be held.

The moment of silence was deafening. The building seemed to darken as onerous black clouds enveloped the top ten floors.

Sittinz became E.I.'s new CEO by a vote of three to two. The resignations of the two dissenters were accepted at the next meeting and four new board members, hand picked by Vincente Vittori, were selected to replace those retired, dead and disenfranchised.

Emrae International's fate was sealed. Dracula was now in charge of the blood bank.

Chapter Twelve

Aboard Air Force One

President Hage was kibitzing with members of the White House press corp in the back of Air Force One. He had just given a major policy speech on the fight against international terrorism during a lunch attended by most of the nation's governors in the convention center in downtown Los Angeles. Due to the time change between the east and west coasts, he was also able to attend a fundraiser breakfast at the Century Plaza Hotel in Century City.

He was a master at the care and feeding of the press. He knew they had to do their jobs and report both sides of most stories. However, he knew it didn't hurt to make friends with as many of them as possible so his side was given just a little more credence.

An aide came racing to the back of the airplane with a message he had just received from the communications room in the upper deck. The President excused himself and walked toward the front of Air Force One. As he passed through the main conference room, he summoned Attorney General Austin to join him in the presidential suite located in the front of the aircraft.

The two entered the office inside the suite and Austin closed the door behind them. "What's up?" asked the Attorney General.

"Good news and bad news from Tropican."

"What do you mean?"

"Phillipe has fled the country. His government was bound to crumble, but to be honest, it came sooner than I ever expected."

"That's great, Mr. President. Your military buildup and threatened invasion destabilized his regime so badly he had to fly the coop. Where'd he go?"

"Don't know. He's still on the move. My guess is Libya. Even though they're trying to be more co-operative with us, they probably won't turn down Phillipe's money."

"You mean Emrae International's money."

"Good point," said the President. "Unfortunately, Roberto Castille has assumed command and declared himself Tropican's new Prime Minister. I think our secret little agreement with him to help us snatch Sittinz in exchange for the release of his drug-running brother from the Federal Pen in Leavenworth gave him a friggin' big head. You were right about the lesser of two evils still being evil."

The room remained silent for several minutes. Austin wasn't about to say "I told you so" and the President was rubbing his forehead trying to find some answer to the surprising new dilemma facing him. Finally, Hage broke the silence. "We've got to find someone to persuade Castille to give it up. We can't allow him to simply continue Phillipe's policies. Who do we know that can be persuasive with him?"

Persuasive, thought Austin. "Hmm, I'll make contact." With that, the AG left the office and went directly to the third deck lounge adjoining the communications room where he could make a private call on Air Force One's untraceable scramble line.

President Hage rocked back in his office chair and put his feet up on the ottoman. He reviewed Austin's prophetic words in his mind. *The lesser of two evils is still evil!*

CHAPTER THIRTEEN

COEUR d'ALENE, IDAHO

A witch holding hands with a skeleton appeared in downtown Coeur d'Alene. They carried sacks to collect their blackmail. Their victims would give up their sweets or face an evil trick. It was Halloween night and kids were out collecting candy. The shops in the Coeur d'Alene Resort Plaza always drew a big crowd. It was an efficient place to trick or treat because the shops were close to each other, plus it was warm inside.

Three well-dressed men in Armani suits walked away from the noise of the Plaza across the Sky Bridge to the Resort so they could talk in private. They walked through the lobby and passed an enormous fireplace roaring with warmth.

When they reached the front desk they turned right and entered Whispers, the Resort's quiet bar. This was no ordinary gin mill; it was a plush and cozy place. Drinks were concocted at a bar located on the upper portion of the two levels configuring the room. Guests had the option of sitting at the bar itself or in more private vignettes where they could talk more confidentially.

As had been their practice for the past week, the trio chose a love seat and two blue comfy chairs surrounding a coffee table. They were tucked in the lower section of Whispers, and the group's leader sat in the love seat facing a glowing fireplace. The glass firebox sat on brown-speckled granite and a gleaming copper chimney floated above. They could see the bartender but the flame and glass veiled their conversation. This had become their war room.

Messieurs Douglas, Demerelli and Stone were the attorneys for the defense. They were good. In fact, they were among the very best in the country at defending guilty people and achieving acquittal. Don Vincent Vittori made sure Curtis Sittinz would have the finest representation possible to secure his freedom and safeguard Vittori's dirty little secret.

To this point, there wasn't any suspicion that his underworld organization was involved in the collapse of Emrae. Vittori wanted to keep it that way and spared no expense in his quest to do so. Vittori's personal attorney, Anthony Cordero, had hand-picked the three pettifoggers and was their sole communications link. Of course, there would never be any direct communication with the Don himself. As always, Cordero served as a layer of protection separating Vittori from connection to crimes of any kind.

Douglas, the head of the group, was from New York City. His representation of lowlife clients over many years had made him a wealthy man. He was sixty-one but looked younger even with his mostly graying hair. He was an impeccable dresser and his grooming was precise, right down to his manicured fingernails. He was not part of a large law firm but handled his clients privately with the help of his stable of three administrative assistants, two full-time law clerks and one paralegal. His offices overlooked Central Park. The Plaza Hotel was his social headquarters, along with the Pheasant Club at the Waldorf and several private country clubs upstate. For him, defending crime paid, and paid handsomely.

Demerelli and Stone were on loan from the Chicago firm of Benston, Greene, Dimarco and Stevenson. They were both tops in their field. They were well-versed in the law but even better versed in how to circumvent it. Demerelli was a graduate of the Harvard School of

Law and Stone matriculated at Yale. However, the most valuable part of their real education came after graduation. Their new law firm provided them with an extensive indoctrination in the science of acquittal of the guilty. They were housed in the prestigious John Hancock Building and from there the entire troupe of legal scholars could look down on all the people of the Windy City.

Vittori's private counsel, Anthony Cordero, was well acquainted with Douglas and the Chicago firm. He had used their services before with excellent results. The Benston Group had specially selected Demerelli and Stone for this important and profitable assignment. The duo had independently learned to excel in graft, deception, and frustrating justice. Both were in their late thirties and had extremely promising futures in deceit.

The three attorneys discussed the jury panel that had been called to the Kootenai County Courthouse to serve in the trial of their client, Curtis Sittinz. One hundred ordinary citizens of the Coeur d'Alene area had been summoned for duty. Now it was the responsibility of the defense and the prosecution to select twelve jurors and two alternates. This jury was exceptionally important because of the high profile of the case and the fact that the President of the United States had given it new tribunal authority. They would have more leeway than a grand jury and the power of a judge to impose a sentence.

Voir dire of the jury panel members had been extremely contentious. Possible jurists had been thoroughly investigated by counsel for the plaintiff and defendant. Those persecuted during the Inquisition had been treated better than this panel. Every little detail of their lives, public, private, and pillow talk was brutally scrutinized. Both sides of the table had used their preemptory challenges liberally during the original questioning cross, and endless re-cross, examinations of the potential jurors. The prosecution had one preemptory left but the defense had used all of theirs and could rely upon only cause to excuse a potential juror. There were only sixteen people remaining, just two more than would be empanelled as the official jurors and alternates.

"Let's review once more the questionnaires of the potential jurors to determine what cause could be possible if we want to get rid of one or two of them," suggested Stone.

"Fine," answered the chief defender Douglas, "but what we're really looking for is who are our best targets to . . . well to . . . convince to vote for our client's innocence with information that we can present outside of court, if you know what I mean."

"Let's cut through the BS," scolded Demerelli. "What we're looking for is who in hell we can blackmail to make sure Sittinz goes free. All we need is one. Even with this tribunal crap, the jury's decision has to be unanimous to convict."

The jury consultants for the defense weren't profiling for I.Q., E.Q., sensitivity or any other attribute. They were profiling for someone who had something to hide. The jury consultants had done an excellent job of investigating private information about the potential jury members. Two of the remaining panelists were still on the potentials list, Nikki Fargo and Violet Hemming. They had identified five possibles and three probables from the original one hundred. Fargo was a probable and Hemming a possible. Tomorrow, in court, the defense would have to do everything in their power to retain both of them. By tomorrow night the jury would be seated, then sequestered at the Coeur d'Alene Resort. The Resort, not court, was where the defense would have to present their convincing evidence–evidence that had nothing to do with their client or case.

They only needed to persuade one.

CHAPTER FOURTEEN

THE PENTHOUSE OF McEUEN TERRACE CONDOMINIUMS

"I made reservations at the Beachouse Restaurant overlooking the lake tonight for us," yelled Betty Hanson to her husband Earl who was outside on the patio. Since she and Earl won the lottery, Betty cooked a whole lot less than she did at their former home in Chicago.

"Great, I like that place," hollered Earl. He was an agreeable easygoing sort and he loved his wife and their little adopted daughter, Helen. "Particularly, their prime rib."

Earl knew good beef. He had worked at the Windy City Packing Company in Chicago for twenty-five years before good fortune struck them with their big lottery win. After paying their taxes, they still had a whopping eighty million left. They invested twenty-five million for their share in Resort Associates along with Clint Diamond, Veronica Whitcomb, Senator Carl Wilder, and Jack Bradley. The Associates borrowed the rest on favorable terms thanks to Senator Wilder's banking connections.

Betty and Earl kept fifteen million for spending money to buy their condo and other goodies. Happily, their home in Chicago, modest as it was, sold for almost enough to pay for their penthouse. The Hanson's invested the remaining forty million dollars in very safe income-producing stocks and securities that generated nearly two million dollars each year with virtually no risk. They knew their strategy was ultra-conservative but they slept well at night knowing their nest egg was secure.

Betty handled the day-to-day household finances while, rock-solid A. G. Edwards and Company managed their overall investments.

"Earl, there must be something wrong with your pension statement from Windy City Packing," said Betty.

"How so?"

"Well, if I read it right this morning, it says you have less than ninety thousand dollars in it. You know, honestly, I haven't paid much attention to it for the past couple of years. With the other money, it didn't seem quite as important as before."

"That can't be right," corrected Earl. "We had several hundred thousand dollars in our 401(k) account. I put in the maximum amount every month and the company matched five per cent of it. You know, we figured we would need that money for retirement."

"I know, you were always a good bread winner and took good care of us. You still do."

Earl picked up the statement from Betty's desk just off the kitchen. Sure enough, it showed a balance of just over eighty-nine thousand dollars. He rifled through the filing cabinet drawers under the desk until he found the 401(k) file. Betty was very well organized and the quarterly statements were in chronological order going back over ten years. When Earl left Windy City Packing, his account balance stood at two hundred and thirty thousand dollars. He studied the statements and realized that the last three quarters had shown a precipitous drop in value. He simply couldn't understand. He was one of thousands of people who paid scant attention to the account.

At the bottom of the account an 800 number was listed to call if there were any questions. Earl picked up the phone and dialed. A recorded voice answered politely and then proceeded to present him with a seemingly unending menu of numbers he could punch in to access information. Finally, in frustration, he hung up and called his friend,

Sandy, in the personnel offices at Windy City Packing.

"Human Resources, how may I direct your call?"

"Yes, is Sandy in today? This is Earl Hanson and I was hoping to speak to her."

"Oh, Mr. Hanson, it is nice to talk to you. I will get her on the line for you." Even though the Hanson's big lottery win had occurred several years ago, they were still the talk of the company. Most people who worked there bought at least one lottery ticket each week, hoping that there was something about working for the meat packing company that was magical and that they would be the next Earl and Betty.

"Earl, it is wonderful to hear from you. We thought you forgot all about us," said Sandy.

"I could never do that. I have lots of friends and many fond memories of that old plant."

The two friends spent several minutes talking about the good old days. Sandy reported that the company was doing okay but that lots of new competition in the marketplace was taking a toll on the bottom line.

"But enough of that. How can I help you?" she asked.

"Betty and I were reading our pension account and I think there is some mistake. I tried to call the 800 number listed on the bottom of the statement but I couldn't seem to get through the jumble of numbers. After being caught in voice mail jail for ten minutes or so I decided to call you and talk to a real human being. I had a nice visit with lots of machines though."

"Oh, that," replied Sandy, completely changing the tone of the conversation from friendly to flat.

Earl didn't respond. He sensed from the sour sound of her voice that maybe there hadn't been an error after all.

Sandy booted her computer and entered Earl's account number. Within seconds the numbers flashed on her monitor. "Eighty-nine thousand, three hundred and five dollars and nine cents," she read aloud as if she were reading the obituaries. "You have been hit just like the rest of us, but not anywhere near as bad."

"What the heck happened?"

"You've been following the Emrae International thing, I assume? I mean the whole world is watching that one. Well, unfortunately our company entrusted our entire pension program to those scoundrels and like thousands of other people, we have taken an enormous hit. Emrae International sold us on a pension program that was all roses and gardenias and what we got was ragweed and dandelions. I'm afraid it is only going to get worse, too."

"Well, it sure can't get much worse."

"You and Betty have actually fared better than most. You would have lost even more except that when you moved to Idaho your losses were reduced. I don't know why, but Idaho is the only state in the country that had some insulation from this terrible debacle. People all over the country from California to Florida, and Washington state to Maine have been hurt. Folks in lots of other countries have felt the pain, too. Most people are being virtually wiped out."

"Oh, my goodness." He wasn't feeling sorry for himself, but for his friends. After all, Betty and he would hardly miss the money.

"Remember Paul Heartly?"

"Sure, how is he?"

"Unfortunately, he is no longer of this world. Last week he blew his brains out because he couldn't handle the financial pain. Joe Blumberg had a fatal heart attack and his wife Wilma is sure it was because of the pension mess."

"Oh, my God Almighty. Sandy, you take my account and turn it over to the rest of the employees. It's only a drop in the bucket but at least they will know Betty and I are with them in spirit. I'll talk to our financial advisors. Maybe we can even help a little more."

"God bless you, Earl. You and Betty are truly wonderful. Thank you from the bottom of our hearts."

Earl slowly hung up the telephone. He stood silently for several moments then turned to his wife. With a heavy heart, he filled Betty in on the terrible financial happenings at Windy City Packing and the tragic loss of their friends. The couple was stunned and could hardly talk.

Betty called the Beachouse and cancelled their reservation. Tonight was not a night to go out on the town. The couple didn't even think about their own misfortune at the hands of Emrae International. Of course, it was true they would hardly miss the pension account, but even if they did their thoughts would be with the others, anyway. Betty and Earl, hand in hand, fell to their knees and prayed for the well-being of their friends and the souls of those so recently departed.

CHAPTER FIFTEEN

COEUR d'ALENE

Curtis Sittinz, who cooked the Emrae books then ran, sat with his cadre of attorneys at the defendant's table in the courtroom. Stone was to his left, with Douglas and Demerelli to his right. Three prosecutors sat across the courtroom and Judge Roger Hammond presided. Twelve jurors and two alternates had finally been selected. It didn't help the defense that the prosecutors used their final preemptory challenge to remove Violet Hemming. Nikki Fargo was seated, but she was an alternate.

The jurors were in their chairs in the jury box. After all the harlotry during voir dire, they seemed excited to get on with it. The numerous recesses, called to allow the judge to castigate both sides in his private chambers for their ferocity, had given the jurors time to get to know each other. After all, they couldn't talk about the case or current events, so about all they could do was talk about themselves. They began to bond and an easy camaraderie developed. It was sort of a one-for-all-and-all-for-one feeling: the twelve musketeers plus two.

Judge Hammond sternly made it clear to the jury that they were not to discuss the proceedings among themselves or with anyone else until they were given the case. The judge instructed the jurors not to read any newspapers, magazines, or books that had not been approved by the bailiffs. Televisions had been removed from the jurors sleeping rooms but the bailiffs would play movies in the jury R & R room. Regular telephones had also been stripped from the rooms and an emergency hotline phone installed. It was connected to the bailiff security room which was already set-up and operational in the Resort. Of course, no cell phones or internet access would be tolerated.

Meals would be eaten at the Resort in a soundproof room. They would be given a menu choice in advance of each meal by the bailiffs. If they wished, they could have a cocktail or two and wine with dinner, but this privilege would be monitored so there was no abuse.

Shit, who's supposed to be in jail here, the bad guys or the jury? I'll bet the defendant who's been denied bail is better treated than we'll be, thought juror number twenty-four William Payton. He worked as a car salesman for Tom Addis Lake City Ford. He was consistently the top salesman in the firm and was affectionately known as Willy "Wheels" Payton because of his knack at making deals. Well paid as he was, "Wheels" was always short of money. He spent it faster than he made it and lived the high life. The defense had looked carefully at Willy but couldn't put their finger on anything they could use. He didn't make their list.

The jury was composed of seven men and five women. Both alternates were female. In addition to Willy, there were two housewives, a teacher, a retired bank loan officer, and a grocery store checker. The owner of a travel agency had also been selected, along with a custodian from the local North Idaho College, an agent from a realty company, and a sales associate from a bookstore. The band of jurors was rounded out with the selection of an unemployed dot-comer, a farmer, a lumber mill worker, and a part-time boat captain from Lake Coeur d'Alene Cruises.

They were down-to-earth, everyday people who had been entrusted with an enormous decision. Sittinz looked at each juror carefully but most of the jurors kept their eyes trained on the judge. The defense watched Nikki Fargo.

If only she could be on the jury itself and not sit as an alternate, thought Douglas.

When Judge Hammond had completed his instructions he ordered the jury to adjourn and told them one more time not to talk about the case. He stood to leave and the bailiff asked for all to rise out of respect for the fact that the high honorable Judge Hammond was walking out.

As the jury itself left the courtroom, the realtor whispered, "Sittinz is kinda cute, isn't he?"

"Shhh, I don't think I can answer that," shushed the teacher.

The defense team regrouped in their usual spot in Whispers. They were somewhat muted. Knowing the weakness of their case in court they realized they had to find some way to get to at least one juror to insure freedom for Sittinz.

"You gotta give the prosecution credit," admitted Demerelli, "they did a darn good job of wiping out our possibles and probables. Now, we've only got Nikki baby."

"It's damn curious why they used their last free pass to dump Violet Hemming. There would have been no way to get her off for cause and her law enforcement background made her look like a perfect juror for the prosecution," said Stone. "It's almost like they knew what our investigators found out about her past. But that is impossible. They were freaking lucky, I guess."

"I wonder just how much luck was involved," said Douglas.

"What do you mean?"

"I mean just what I said, they cherry-picked our targets perfectly. It's almost as though they have someone inside who knows our every move."

"No way. If that was the case, how come we still got Fargo?"

"They worked like hell to bounce her for cause and couldn't get her thrown out. If I was the judge I couldn't have found cause either. Plus, she's an alternate, not a voter. I'll bet a nickel if they would have had one more preemptory, Nikki Fargo would be home right now with her loving husband or bopping her boyfriend instead of sitting here sequestered."

"I think you're imagining things. Have another drink," said Demerelli.

J. J. Hunter

Douglas was glum as he ordered another Scotch and silently scrutinized the jury by number. Tribunal procedures called for each person ultimately seated in the jury box to be referred to by their original jury panel number to further conceal their identity and to keep the numerical order in the court. "Maybe so, but I've got a nagging feeling there's something or someone out there looking over our shoulder."

CHAPTER SIXTEEN

THE COEUR d'ALENE RESORT

Defense Counselor Douglas had a fitful night's sleep. The red numbers on the clock radio in his room said it was 5:45 AM and he finally decided to get up. It was still dark outside and the sun wouldn't show its light for another half-hour. He opened his door and took the morning copy of *The Coeur d'Alene Press* from the outside knob where it had been hung an hour earlier.

He started the brew cycle of the coffee maker in his room, brushed his teeth, then took the newspaper and read it on the throne.

After he finished the paper, Douglas walked to the patio door and pulled the drape wand to expose a magnificent view of the lake and surrounding mountains. He had admired this view on dozens of mornings, but it was still stunning. He opened the door to the balcony and stepped out in the crisp, clean North Idaho air. He sat on the balcony and drank his coffee as doubts kept nagging him. He made a decision. Douglas walked back into the room, refilled his coffee cup and dialed the phone.

"Law offices of Anthony Cordero," announced the receptionist with a New York accent. The firm was already open due to the three-hour time difference between Coeur d'Alene and Buffalo.

"Good morning, Gloria. This is Bob Douglas. May I please speak to Tony?"

"Of course, Mr. Douglas. I'll get him on the line for you right away."

Douglas took a deep swig of coffee and fidgeted while he waited.

"Good morning, Bob. How is everything in God's country?" asked Cordero.

"It's as beautiful as ever out here, but I barely slept a wink last night."

"How come?"

"Tony, the jury has been seated and we didn't fare to well with our special list of potential jurors," admitted Douglas. He hated reporting this information to Cordero because he knew that when Don Vittori was informed he would be unhappy. It was not healthy for anybody when Vittori was unhappy.

"You told me you thought you had at least two candidates just yesterday. What the hell happened?"

Douglas explained the unexpected preemptory challenge of Violet Hemming by the prosecution and informed Cordero that Nikki Fargo was seated only a non-voting alternate. Anthony was not pleased and pressed Douglas on how such a situation could have happened.

"It's uncanny," Douglas complained. "They seem to know exactly what we're thinking but there's no way they could. I know your special client will be damn concerned when you tell him, but I thought you ought to know so you can communicate the bad news ASAP. We're working on some ideas to get back in the game."

"Back in the game? From the sounds of it you haven't even been in it yet. I'm not about to take the rap on this for you guys. We're paying you good money, lots of good money, and these are the kind of results we get?"

Douglas knew Cordero didn't want an answer to his question and kept quiet.

"Shit! Keep me informed," ordered Cordero as the conversation abruptly ended.

Douglas held the phone in his hand as though it was dead mouse. He stared at it for a couple of seconds after Cordero had hung up on him. "If you think this is so doggoned easy why don't you handle it yourself," said Douglas to the phone. The phone didn't answer.

°Back in Buffalo, Cordero picked up his phone and dialed a very private number. He gave a detailed report on everything Douglas had told him. Cordero was a brave and loyal soldier.

Chapter Seventeen

Kootenai County Courthouse

All rose for the entrance of his sanctimonious honor, Judge Roger Hammond, as Jacob, the courtroom bailiff, hailed his arrival. The judge gaveled the proceedings to order.

Finally, it was show time. Probable cause evidence had been presented in the pretrial hearings. The defendant had his day in court for arraignment and all the wrangling over jurisdictional and tribunal rules was now over. The jury was seated and it was time for the prosecution to prove, beyond a reasonable doubt, that Curtis Sittinz was guilty as charged.

The morning was quickly filled with briefs, arguments, and objections. Both sides made it clear this would not be a friendly encounter.

The Tribunal Order signed by President Hage and finally agreed to by both sides was patterned loosely after the Permanent Court of Arbitration that had been established in 1899 in the Netherlands.

There were some significant deviations, however. The major difference was in the selection and empowerment of the jury. In the

International Court, each member nation has the right to appoint up to four jurors versed in international law. The disputants could then select arbitrators from that panel or agree on an umpire to preside over the hearing.

The umpire in the Emrae International case had already been determined to be Judge Hammond. Instead of The Hague, this trial would be in Coeur d'Alene. Instead of jurists with exceptional knowledge in the laws among nations, these arbitrators would be normal, ordinary Idaho citizens with expertise in good old-fashioned common sense.

Unlike traditional court, the Tribunal Order called for the jury to hold sway over both verdict *and* any subsequent sentencing. The decision of jury would be final with no appeal by the victor or the vanquished.

Opening remarks were surprisingly short by the prosecution and almost nil by the defense. Sittinz's advocates made it clear they would not have to do much in court because the case against their innocent client was totally bogus. It was about all they could say. They played out their part in the courtroom but knew victory wouldn't occur there. Their win would be the result of one vote in the jury deliberation room.

The prosecution, ardent and articulate, opened their case quickly and picked up momentum throughout the presentation. The jury was informed that, not only would the prosecution prove Sittinz's guilt beyond any reasonable doubt; they would prove him guilty beyond the shadow of any doubt, period!

They began by reviewing the sad case of Bob Robinson. The jury was told how this proud custodian, who had worked for Emrae International for almost all of his adult life, had been defrauded by the defendant then, in desperation, turned to suicide. They detailed how Emrae International became a huge success by using legitimate and ethical business practices for years. Then, shortly after Sittinz took control of the company, it turned into a giant monster sucking fortunes from thousands of good people, people just like Bob Robinson.

Douglas, Demerelli and Stone squirmed in their chairs. They watched the eyes of the jury and saw several filled with tears.

The prosecution explained the basics of Emrae International's methods. Under the leadership of Sittinz, the financial giant began to specialize in the world of pension investments. E.I. financial experts invested the pensioners' money in excellent long-term stock investments, which allowed portfolios to grow without creating current tax burdens.

Sittinz and Bronson started cheating Emrae International clients in a small way. When an account executive left the company, his customers were transferred to a new broker. This new broker was a fictitious person who existed in name only and served as an alias for Bronson. He would change the address on the client's true monthly statement to a Post Office Box and then make up a fake statement that was mailed to the client's real address. This technique kept the investor completely in the dark that his account was being manipulated. It worked well and the revenue generated for the two embezzlers was serious money, but not nearly enough to satisfy their lust.

To increase the scope and pace of their larceny, they secretly developed and installed imaginative software they dubbed *boomerang,* which allowed them to cheat clients more efficiently.

Boomerang was housed in a top secret corner office on the seventy-second floor of the Emrae International Tower. It was a perfect location, which allowed Sittinz and Bronson to baby-sit their little one and keep its very existence a secret. Their pride and joy, no latchkey child, was guarded by cameras and alarms twenty-four hours each day. Tiny little green and red lights blinked incessantly as the system guided stocks and bonds back and forth among thousands of client accounts. It was an enormously effective system, primarily developed by Bronson, who was a true savant in the computer world. His substantial software knowledge allowed him to tap *boomerang* into the main computer systems within Emrae without the knowledge of any other Emrae personnel.

The company converted accounts from traditional pension plans to new cash balance plans. This change alone allowed Emrae to pay out less to older workers because the new plan was more front-loaded. At the same time Emrae instituted a staggered quarterly statement cycle. Instead of statements mailed to all clients at the end of each calendar quarter, they were staggered on a fiscal basis through the quarter with just under eight per cent of the clients receiving their statement at the conclusion of each week. Emrae explained this procedure was implemented as a cost-saving measure to keep overhead down and allow staff members and equipment to even out the workload. By keeping their costs down, the company would be able to generate more profit for shareholders and value for customers.

Within twenty-four hours after the client statement was printed and mailed showing the correct ending balance, *boomerang* removed one half of the shares in the account. Just fewer than twenty per cent of these shares were used to cover the shortages in other customer accounts.

The balance of the temporarily embezzled account would be churned in the marketplace. Emrae traders were among the best in the business. Their legitimate business models were used to sell stock short if they felt the price was going down and buy it back a month or two later at a lower price. The computer software would automatically bounce the proper number of shares back to the original client account in time for that statement to be printed and mailed. The top brass at Emrae would collect the difference between the higher-priced stock at the beginning of the cycle and the lower-priced stock that replaced it.

Even when stock went up in a quarter it didn't usually do so in a straight line and Emrae cashed in on the daily ups and downs of each stock. Sure, they guessed wrong and lost many times but the odds were on their side just like blackjack or roulette favors the house in Las Vegas. The margins on each individual account were fairly small but the billions of dollars churning through the Emrae traders resulted in a huge cache of cash that was electronically transferred to secret accounts in Tropican.

In the beginning, the con artists targeted people who had at least ten years before retirement. These were clients that had retirement on their mind but wouldn't be cashing in for a few more years and would be less likely to discover Emrae's balance sheet roulette. Instead of kiting checks, Sittinz and Bronson kited stock.

The prosecution painstakingly showed how the scheme allowed billions of dollars to be siphoned off without detection. If a client decided to sell then his account was fully funded and the embezzlers simply had to give back a little of the fat. In fact, such examples were used as testimonials in Emrae advertising. Thousands and thousands of unknowing clients simply let their accounts grow quietly and untouched as they prepared for their later years. Their statements were comforting and few questions were asked.

The prosecution stipulated that even Sittinz knew such a plan could only last a short time before it was discovered. That didn't matter because there was plenty of time to steal a king's ransom and then abscond with it, just as Sittinz did by running off to Tropican. They admitted that Sittinz's cohort, Andrew Bronson, had so far successfully evaded capture by the authorities, but assured the jury that he, too, would be brought to tribunal justice.

All in all, the prosecution was convincing and their witnesses and evidence compelling. The defense objected over and over. Once they even objected to their own objection. Judge Hammond overruled time and time again. The lead prosecutor informed the jury that over the next few weeks they would be presenting credible evidence of many more stories just like that of poor Bob Robinson. The defense team believed them.

Barristers Douglas, Demerelli and Stone sat in their usual cushy blue chairs in Whispers until closing. They were drinking very heavily.

CHAPTER EIGHTEEN

THE COEUR d'ALENE RESORT

Defense attorney Douglas was experiencing the ultimate horror as an assassin rushed at him holding a long knife high over his head. The sharp point of the blade started its downward motion heading directly between the attorney's eyes, just above the bridge of his nose. Douglas wished he was dreaming.

God, he thought, *I'm doing the best I can to save their client but we have absolute nothing to base any kind of tangible legal defense on. I told Cordero that when he hired us.*

From the time he first saw the knife, until it struck, seemed like an eternity. He was Catholic and tried to blurt an Act of Contrition to save him from final damnation. There wasn't enough time. He raised his arms over his face to protect himself. He jerked his head to the right.

Why have you sent this mad Sicilian to kill me, Cordero?

He ducked his head to the left. The knife struck!

At that moment Douglas's eyes opened wide. The morning sun was shining through the window and his arms were flailing over his head. He was safe in his room at The Coeur d'Alene Resort. His dream was a terrible nightmare, after all.

Douglas sat up in his bed, a bed soaked with sweat.

"Oh God," he said out loud, "thank you!" He rolled out of bed and headed for the bathroom. He had peed his pants so he took off the wet underwear and wiped himself with a moist towel. He picked up the phone in the bathroom to call Cordero. He hadn't even touched one number on the keypad when he hung up. He rubbed his face with his hands. *Get a grip!*

After showering and composing himself, Douglas called his two cohorts and ordered them to meet him in twenty minutes at Dockside, the Resort's lobby level restaurant overlooking the lake. Thirty minutes later an unshaven Demerelli arrived and ten minutes after that Stone appeared on the scene.

"What the hell is so pressing this early in the morning? I don't even like breakfast," groused Stone. "I wish I was still in bed."

"If wishes were horses, we'd all be riders," jabbed Demerelli in an effort to get Stone's goat.

"We're going to get blown out of court," blurted Douglas. "When that happens, there is a real possibility our employer will consider us expendable, very expendable. Sittinz is guilty as sin and the whole world knows it."

"Gentlemen are you ready to order?" asked Jasmine who, even early in the morning, was bright and bubbly.

"Oh, yes ma'am," said Demerelli. "What do you recommend young lady?"

"JD is working the grill and he specializes in his grandfather's secret recipe of goulash." Jasmine could see from the unshaven look of Demerelli and the bloodshot eyes of Stone that goulash would be perfect to soak up the residue of alcohol from the night before.

"Goulash?" questioned Douglas. "We've already lived through Halloween here in Coeur d'Alene. Is it ghoulish goulash?"

"No," responded Jasmine with a big smile, "It is good goulash. Trust me, you will love JD's specialty."

"Okay, let's go with goulash all around the table," decided Douglas. The others nodded in agreement.

Jasmine went back to the kitchen after pouring three cups of steaming hot coffee and leaving a pot on the table to help relieve hangovers. JD began cracking eggs and adding them to the other ingredients of his secret family recipe.

"So, boss, did you just come to the startling conclusion that we don't have a tinker's damn of a case?" asked Demerelli.

"Don't screw with me. This is a very serious situation. It's obvious we're in big difficulty in court." Douglas continued, "Our chance in court is about as good as a Chihuahua becoming a Seeing Eye dog."

Stone and Demerelli sat up in their chairs, seeming to realize just how passionate their boss had become.

Douglas continued his ranting. "You know very well that our client's backer is nobody to fool around with. There's a slow burn smoldering in Buffalo right now. I've kept Cordero fully informed and you can count on the fact that he has kept you-know-who fully briefed."

"He's got to realize we've got next to nothing to work with," countered Stone.

"He isn't one bit interested in what we've got to work with. He is interested in winning, period. He doesn't care how we accomplish our assignment, but you can bet the farm he expects no less than complete vindication for Sittinz." Douglas's voice trailed off. His message was pathetically accurate.

"A slow burn, huh?" repeated Stone.

"Yeah, just like the kind you see on the fuse of a stick of dynamite right before it blows," droned Demerelli with a somber look on his face.

"No shit, Sherlock," said Douglas.

Jasmine delivered breakfast and another helping of her infectious smile. The trio ate in silence, their mood as dark as the overcast sky. Douglas suffered a flashback of his nightmare and saw the sharp pointed switchblade heading for his eyes.

It's come down to one chance and one chance only. We have got to find a way to get Nikki Fargo on the jury panel.

CHAPTER NINETEEN

THE COEUR d'ALENE RESORT SPA

It was late Saturday afternoon. There was no court because of the weekend. Douglas looked out the windows of the Resort spa's meditation room where he rested between treatments. There was only one other person relaxing in the room. The person was completely covered, head to toe, with towel wraps and appeared to be sleeping so he couldn't tell if it was a she or a he.

Douglas's eyes moved from the dancing flames of the room's fireplace to the windows overlooking the lake and mountains outside. The first snowfall of the winter season had turned the pine trees and mountains into a beautiful white mosaic. Steam rose from the lake because the water temperature was warmer than the outside air. It was a tranquil, magnificent sight.

Douglas wore a bathrobe and slippers. He had just completed a forty-five minute aromatherapy mineral bath in the spa's hydrotherapy tub. The German Kerstin Florian crystals the therapist had added to the hot water in the tub were the perfect revitalizing combination to relieve the tension from weeks of courtroom stress.

Douglas purposely left more time than normal between his first treatment and his upcoming hot stone massage. He read the jury questionnaires and summaries for the umpteenth time hoping the inspiration for a successful idea to remove one of them would somehow hit him like a lightning bolt.

The peaceful aromatherapy bath had relaxed him. He was already worn-out from the strain of the courtroom, the worry over his own well being, and the fact that for the past weeks he had been only able to sleep in installments. He had not been able to have the benefit of even one full night of deep sleep since this whole mess had begun. His eyelids started to droop.

His snooze was interrupted when the bundle of towels laying on the padded teakwood chaise lounge next to him started to move. The gender mystery was soon solved as the towels, slowly pulled up from the person's feet, revealed perfectly manicured toes and the most beautifully shaped feminine legs that Douglas had ever remembered seeing. The woman slowly removed the towels covering her top half.

She had beautiful flowing black hair that reminded him of delicate silk from a spinning wheel. Her movement caused her bathrobe to pull open, exposing her chest. The opening didn't bare all, but just enough cleavage for Douglas to realize that this was one damn well-put-together woman. He noticed her bright red finger nail polish as she reached up to remove the large cotton pads that covered and soothed her eyes.

"Oh," she said as she fully covered her chest with her bathrobe and arms, "I didn't realize there was somebody else here in the meditation room."

"Forgive me, I didn't mean to startle you," apologized the attorney embarrassed that his gawking was now obvious. He looked away, fingered the papers he had been reading earlier and cleared his throat.

As the blur in her eyes caused by the cotton cleared she recognized Douglas as a frequent guest of the hotel. "Oh, I know you. You've been staying here regularly for the past several months."

She reached out her hand to greet the attorney and his heart melted as he embraced her palm. "I am Robert Douglas," he stuttered.

"Of course you are," she said admiringly. "I am Veronica Whitcomb and this is my Resort. It's nice to see you here in my spa. I've noticed you before with your business associates in Whispers."

"Oh, yes, Whispers is a favorite of ours."

She really wasn't listening and prattled on. "The spa staff here so much enjoys having me come in. When they give me various treatments they always compliment my perfect muscle tone and figure. I really think it's a treat for them to be able to work on me and I must say our spa is one of the best. I have experienced spas throughout the Americas and Europe. Ours is not the biggest by any means, but I think it is one of the nicest."

"Mr. Douglas we are ready for your hot stone massage?" asked masseuse Jennelle as she opened the door to the meditation room.

Before Douglas could answer Whitcomb interrupted, "Oh, you will love the stone massage. It's one of the best in the world. You'll see. It's a total out-of-body experience. It will give you feelings you've never felt before."

"Thank you Mrs. Whitcomb. It was an honor to meet you. Hopefully, I will have the pleasure again soon."

"Yes, that would be delicious."

"And, of course I am ready," acknowledged the lawyer to the therapist as he stuffed the jury documents in his briefcase. He locked the latches and carried it with him as he followed Jennelle to the treatment room.

As Jennelle began the treatment she explained that the stones had been carefully selected. They were rounded and very smooth. "Many guests of the spa who have experienced the treatment have commented that it's a wonderful body and mind experience. Some Native American tribes, particularly those who lived along flowing rivers, discovered the magic of the rocks years ago."

"Interesting," whispered Douglas. He spoke the word slowly. He was already beginning to relax into a deep trance.

"The river was water and water was life itself," she explained. Her voice was softer now to allow her client to become deeply relaxed. "These uniquely shaped stones were highly valued in the tribal culture. When people from the spirit world returned to relax by the river they would lay their heads on such stones as they rested by the river of life.

In other words, they served as pillows for the spirits of the ancestors. In this way, their vision and wisdom had been transferred to the rocks."

Jennelle was very pleasant with soft hands and a soothing voice. Douglas lay on his stomach with his head supported by the massage table's face cradle. Smooth heated stones were placed up and down his spine and he felt their warmth deep in his tissue.

Jennelle massaged him with hot stones she held in the palms of her hands. He grunted in delight a few times and nearly fell asleep. His eyes were closed and he could envision running water and a rainbow of colors. As if by magic, the idea he had been seeking mysteriously came to him. Not like a lightning bolt, but like a slow moving sensation, the same sensation the hot stones created deep in the tissues of his body. The inspiration had been hiding in his mind but no amount of tossing and turning the night before could break it loose.

Douglas quickly sat up on the massage table with the sheet covering him.

"Oh, Mr. Douglas, did I hurt you?"

"On the contrary, young lady. Your hot stone massage has helped me realize the answer to a dilemma that has been troubling me for quite some time. Your treatment was perfect but I must go back to my room straight away and place a call."

"You're sure everything is okay?" she asked.

"Perfect. Never felt better."

Jennelle left the room so that he could dress in his bathrobe and slippers privately. He grabbed his briefcase. The hot stones had stimulated him all right, both body and mind. Douglas signed the bill and left Jennelle a generous tip. He gave her a hug of gratitude as he hurried from the spa and literally ran to his room.

Cordero answered his home phone at the third ring with a flat voice, "Yes?"

"Anthony, this is Bob Douglas and the answer to our prayers has just hit me."

"I'm all ears, let's hear it."

"Juror number thirty-nine."

"What the hell about juror number thirty-nine?"

"She owns her own travel agency and loves to travel. She noted in her juror questionnaire that she's been unable to take any trips lately because her father died last year and her eighty-three year old mother has dementia. She's her mother's only child." Douglas was speaking fast with enthusiasm in his voice. "The mother lives alone on their farm out in the boonies. Juror thirty-nine tried to get excused because she was so worried about her but the good judge would hear nothing of it."

"What does all of this have to do with our problem?" pressed Cordero.

"You get your boss to order his goons to go and take her for a ride and make her disappear. It's obvious good old number thirty-nine loves her mother very much. When she hears she's walked off by herself, to God knows where, and is lost, she'll hit the panic button and Judge Hammond will have to let thirty-nine go find her mother."

"You mean we knock off an old lady?"

"Hell no. Don't you understand? The mother's got a bad case of Alzheimer's. As soon as thirty-nine is excused from the jury, the thugs make her reappear. She can tell 'em what happened in 1929 but can't remember what happened yesterday. She'll never remember where she went or who took her there. It's perfect. No muss, no fuss."

"I'll call for authorization," said Cordero. "And I'll make sure Santino knows the rules on this one. We don't need to hurt a harmless old lady."

Thoroughly satisfied, Douglas hung up the phone and realized he was shaking with excitement. He looked down at the spa slippers he was still wearing.

I shudda had that hot rocks massage weeks ago!

CHAPTER TWENTY

TROPICAN CITY

The streets of the capitol city of Tropican were wall-to-wall people waiting for the inaugural parade of their new Prime Minister Roberto Castille to pass by. The crowds cheered because Louis Phillipe had fled their island nation. The forced cheers and chants for the new Prime Minister were due the thousands of soldiers standing throughout the parade route carrying threatening AK-47s.

Oliver Mustavio had driven a taxi in Tropican City for twenty years. His cab was a white minivan with black tires, no hubcaps, dark tinted windows and the word TAXI written in bold black letters. All cab drivers were required to have their picture, name, and license number in a clear plastic holder on the dashboard of their cab. Most put a picture of their children in the same plastic holder because it helped generate tips. Oliver had a picture of his wife Rosita and his two children, Jossepe and Maria, because of his love for them. Throughout each day, he would look at his family and remember that his hard work was for them. A bright red rosary hung from his rear view mirror representing his deep faith in God.

But this day, the taxi driver and his family were in grave danger.

During the middle of the night, two desperate men burst into the tiny Mustavio home and held all four of them hostage. Rosita, Jossepe and Maria were kept inside the house at gunpoint by one of the intruders and the other forced Oliver to drive him to downtown Tropican City.

"Travel just under the speed limit and do not attract any attention," the man ordered. He held an automatic pistol and sat on the floor directly behind the frightened taxi driver. The back seats of the cab had been removed and replaced by a mound of explosives. They were wired to a dead man switch that would detonate the pile ten seconds after it was released. The kidnapper held down the switch with the thumb of his left hand.

Two tourists tried to hail the cab but Oliver ignored them as instructed. "Why are you doing this?" Oliver asked.

"Shut up and do exactly as I say. Do not ask any questions if you wish to save your family. Turn left on Tropican Avenue and drive toward Atlantic Street."

"We're going to the center of downtown?"

"I said to shut up."

Oliver kept his mouth closed. His rosary swung back and forth as he maneuvered the van along the narrow bumpy road. He looked at the picture of his family while he begged and prayed to God that they would be safe. Oliver glanced in the rear view mirror and could see his captor's thumb still holding the dead man switch. Mustavio served as a conscript in the Tropican Brigade when he was a young man and understood such a weapon. He had used one once under orders and was an eyewitness to its deadly effects. He regretted that terrible incident but was powerless to change history. He pledged to God that he would never kill again even if ordered to do so.

The intersection of Tropican Avenue and Atlantic Street created a broad plaza. *Good,* thought Oliver, *the people watching the parade will not be hurt if the explosives go off in the middle of the intersection. I will not crash this taxi into the crowd.*

"Pick up speed now and drive right through the barrier blocking the plaza."

My God, this crazy terrorist is going to try and make me blow up hundreds of my fellow citizens.

He peeked in his rear view mirror. His rosary was swinging wildly now. The lunatic still had is thumb on the switch. Oliver looked at the picture of his family. This time he would not follow orders to kill but would drive the cab into the fountain in the middle of the plaza where it could do little damage. If he was lucky, he too could jump clear of the cab before it exploded then run home to save his family. He sat high enough in his seat to see that the center of the plaza was empty and was emboldened that his plan would work.

He took one more look into the rear view mirror as the taxi hit the wooden barrier. His captor released the dead man switch and jumped from the vehicle. Oliver swerved around the crowd. At that split second, the limousine carrying Prime Minister Castille turned directly into the path that Oliver had chosen. He pulled the emergency brake. It snapped off in his hand. He slammed the foot brake but the pedal went all the way to the floor. The break fluid line had been cut.

They knew all along I would turn away from the crowd. They timed it perfectly to kill Castille. Oliver looked at the picture of his family as the taxi slammed into the limousine.

The bomb was designed to cause severe damage in a very small area. It worked perfectly. The Prime Minister was killed instantly, but not a single person in the crowd was hurt.

The man guarding Oliver's family received a radio message in his earpiece. He instantly ran from the Mustavio home without saying a word. Rosita, Joseppe and Maria would never know that Oliver had paid the ultimate price for a mistake he had made under orders many years earlier.

The gunman from the taxi walked briskly from the downtown plaza. When he was about a block away he punched a series of numbers into his cell phone.

"Yes?" answered a woman.

"It is done."

Antoinette said nothing. She allowed herself a slight smile comforted in the thought that Castille had finally been eliminated. Her lips stiffened as she closed the cover on her cell phone.

Finally, it is over.

CHAPTER TWENTY-ONE

THE OFFICE OF THE ATTORNEY GENERAL OF THE UNITED STATES, WASHINGTON, D.C.

It was raining hard in the District of Columbia as the lead prosecutor in the Emrae International trial, James Hart, and his two rain-soaked assistants dashed into the gray concrete Justice Building. Just before they entered the front doors they glanced up at the words etched into the concrete above, "JUSTICE — IS — THE — GREAT — INTEREST — OF — MAN — ON — EARTH. WHEREVER — HER — TEMPLE — STANDS — THERE — IS — A— FOUNDATION — FOR — SOCIAL — SECURITY — GENERAL — HAPPINESS — AND — THE — IMPROVEMENT — AND — PROGRESS — OF — OUR — RACE."

In spite of the tightened security of the building, they were greeted in the lobby by the Solicitor General himself and whisked directly to the office of Attorney General Austin. The five people exchanged greetings and the three prosecutors removed their wet raincoats and hung them on the coat stand to drip dry.

It was the weekend and the nation's chief law enforcement officer was not wearing his usual blue pinstriped suit and starched white shirt and tie. He was more casual with a blue Cutter & Buck polo shirt and white vest. Solicitor General Davis came suited up, as did the three visitors.

The quintet took their places around a large mahogany conference table and settled into comfortable Stickley chairs that the A.G. had personally ordered when President Hage first appointed him to office. His confirmation hearings had been nasty and the political opposition led by Senator Carl Wilder of Idaho was merciless. However, the President put all of his prestige on the line for his former college fraternity brother and after three ballots in the Senate, on a fifty-one to forty-nine near party-line vote, the upper chamber finally confirmed Austin. The Senator from Austin's home state finally crossed the aisle to vote for his fellow North Carolinian. The A.G. had done a credible job in office and even the curmudgeon Wilder had swung support his way on several issues. None were more important, however, than the Emrae International situation that dogged the entire country.

Diet Mountain Dew and Coke were served, along with one of Austin's favorites, microwave popcorn.

"Okay, let's get down to business," ordered the Attorney General as he stuffed a fistful of popcorn into his mouth and gulped a swig of Coke.

The prosecutors didn't officially work for the Solicitor General, who reported to the A.G. The agreement with the defense counsel called for independent prosecutors. The Solicitor General had agreed to those conditions on paper, but the reality was that the prosecutors danced to the tune of the Solicitor.

Chief Prosecutor Hart started the discussion. "We are faring very well at this point, gentlemen. We have presented damning testimony over and over and our jury consultant says we're hitting all the right buttons. There have been so many tears in the jury box that the courthouse janitor doesn't have to fill his bucket with water to mop at night. I think we're really pasting them but good. The defense doesn't know whether to wind their butts or scratch their watches."

"Our first Attorney General Edmund Randolph, who served under George Washington, would be turning over in his grave if he knew how involved we are in this Emrae shit. But, President Hage has really zeroed in on this one. He wants that lying Sittinz and his cronies brought to justice big time."

"Randolph might not be as uncomfortable as you think, Mr. Attorney General. After all, our department's main job is to protect the public interest. Certainly, we're trying to safeguard consumers who have been screwed by Emrae. George Washington probably had ol' Eddy boy pull a few fast ones too," comforted the Solicitor General.

"Maybe so," said Austin.

"Plus, as Solicitor General, I assign attorneys to argue before the Supreme Court of the United States so we certainly should be able to give a little input to a group of patriotic prosecutors fighting it out with a lousy bunch of crooks in an Idaho court."

"Whether we're on solid ground doesn't matter now because we are in it up to our necks. We probably crossed the line by trying to coach Judge Hammond in Kootenai County. He sure as hell thinks he's some sort of little feudal god out there. His honor certainly considers himself above federal laws, that's for sure," said the Attorney General.

"He's been pretty good so far," countered Hart. "I don't think he cares much for Sittinz and his crooked lawyers."

"Speaking of crooked, we winked an eye or two at the scales of justice with our little plant in the jury panel," said Solicitor Davis.

"You needn't worry about that. I'm absolutely confidant our mole will never say a single word about our . . . well, our little strategy."

"I hope like hell you're right, Jim," said Davis.

"I'll have one more little chit-chat with Jane Doe before we rest our case, but there is absolutely nothing to be concerned about."

"Nothing?"

"Well, the bailiffs did find a cell phone in the room of a juror by the name of William Payton. Cell phones are forbidden and we're not sure where he got it," admitted Hart.

"I assume you checked out if any calls were made from it," asked Davis.

"Of course we did. A couple were made to Lake City Ford where he works and one was made to a number that we haven't been able to track down at the moment," said Hart's senior assistant. "It seems to be a shielded number of some type that relays through several constantly changing digital numbers. We're on it and also checking the Ford dealership phone records to make sure he wasn't transferred through their switchboard to some other number. I've got to admit I don't exactly trust slick Willy."

"You damn well better make sure he's not on the take," ordered Davis.

The five discussed the case for another thirty minutes. The prosecutors gave assurance that on the merits of the trial, there was no way Sittinz would go free. Austin and Davis gave the trio of prosecutors the latest intelligence they had regarding Emrae and up-to-the-minute results of the FBI investigation of the gritty little details of the case.

The Attorney General and Solicitor General cautioned the prosecutors one more time to keep a close eye on the jury. Their impartiality was essential to the successful conclusion of this incredibly complex case. It was critical to the well-being of the entire nation that every safety measure be taken to insure a vote of guilty, which would result in a stiff sentence.

The meeting was coming near an end when the chief prosecutor asked, "Have you got anything else for us before we head back out west?"

"One other little tidbit," chipped in Attorney General Austin. "My Criminal Division has stumbled onto a little intelligence that just might become pertinent in this case. During racketeering-based wiretaps authorized by a New York federal court, some very interesting information resulted from our legal eavesdropping. Sittinz may end up becoming bait for a much bigger fish, but we're not ready to name names just yet. This is just a word to the wise. Keep your eyes wide open for any clues regarding just who might have been working behind the scenes with Sittinz."

"You mean Andrew Bronson, the fancy flimflam bookkeeper, I presume," said one of the assistant prosecutors with an air of confidence.

"No, I do not. We will find Bronson and take care of him in due time. However, if our tap pans out we may be able to invoke some RICO Statutes to reel in an enormous whale. Bronson is a minnow and Sittinz's a small tuna compared to this Moby Dick. I can't say more right now but keep your ears to the ground," ordered Austin as he stood to signal an end to the meeting.

"Attorney General Austin," inquired Hart as he put on his coat, "may I take the liberty of asking you a sensitive question before we go?"

"You can ask but I may not respond. What is it?"

"Does Foggy Bottom or President Hage know about our little sit-down today and our mole on the jury panel?"

"You know you insult me by asking such a question. The State Department has absolutely no knowledge of any of this and I could never answer such an impertinent question about our Commander in Chief."

"Yes sir, I am sorry," responded the repentant prosecutor with his head lowered in shame.

Austin smiled and, after a couple of moments, slowly nodded his head up and down. "But, I would deny I ever said it."

Hart and his associates smiled back and left the A.G.'s office comforted in the knowledge their mission had the highest approval in the land. The three prosecutors exited the Justice Building, dodged the raindrops and puddles and jumped in a cab for Washington-Dulles International Airport to catch their flight back to Coeur d'Alene.

"They sound quite confident," said Davis.

"That they do," agreed Austin. "I just hope Senator Wilder knew what he was talking about when he told the President that an Idaho jury would fry Sittinz's ass."

CHAPTER TWENTY-TWO

CRUISING ON LAKE COEUR d'ALENE

The jury had been sequestered for nearly six weeks. There had been no serious problems and everyone seemed to be getting along well. The bailiffs were pleasantly surprised.

The prosecution was not expected to rest its case for at least another week and then nobody knew for sure how many months the defense would rattle on.

The bailiffs had made arrangements with Jack Bradley, general manager of the Resort, for a cruise on one of the excursion boats of Lake Coeur d'Alene Cruises. The Resort featured the *North Pole Holiday in Lights* program every winter season, which officially started with a gala fireworks show the Friday after Thanksgiving. The bailiffs felt it was only fair to give the jury a little freedom and take them on an excursion to see Santa. Even big kids liked to go to the North Pole.

Bradley offered the boat on a complimentary basis and left the lights up longer than normal to accommodate his special sequestered guests. It was his way of saying thanks to the bailiffs for the nice piece of off-season business that they had sent his way.

Captain Franklin Dinning greeted the jurors and bailiffs as they boarded the *Coeur d'Alene*. Along with the *Mish-An-Nock*, it was the largest of the fleet's six vessels. Peter Harding, the Resort's director of food and beverage, went on the cruise to assist his friend, Captain Dinning, host their special guests. The jurors seemed excited.

The normal cruise to the North Pole lasted about an hour. However, tonight's special cruise of the court would include dinner and a more extensive excursion around the lakeshore that would last three hours. The bailiffs backed off the tight security for the evening. After all, the group was getting along nicely and they were totally isolated from the public because the cruise was a private charter.

The bailiffs didn't have to worry about anyone in their custody walking off the boat in the middle of the lake. Plus, a sheriff's marine patrol boat would closely follow the *Coeur d'Alene* to make sure no other boats approached the vessel during the journey. Once all were on board and accounted for, the caged group had full run of the ship. However, they did make sure that none of the jurors, particularly Willy "Wheels" Payton, had any possible access any of the boat's communication gear. Upon return later in the evening, the bailiffs would re-establish their strict rules.

Cocktails were served during the first half-hour of the cruise followed by a turkey and ham buffet. After dinner the jurors were allowed to move freely around the boat. The entire group, except for one person, stayed on the lower deck out of the cold weather. Several jurors engaged in a game of gin rummy while others simply relaxed and enjoyed the trip. The bailiffs sat together playing a game of chess.

Nikki Fargo went outside and hurried up the aft stairway on the port side leading to the upper deck. She knew exactly where she was headed. She made a beeline for the captain's private quarters located behind the wheelhouse. When she reached the door it instantaneously swung open and she fell into the waiting arms of Peter Harding. They shared a deep, intimate kiss. He wrapped his arms around her and they fell to the couch in the captain's personal hideaway.

Nikki was married. Peter never had been. They had known each other for nearly seventeen years. In fact, before Nikki married and moved to Coeur d'Alene, she worked in the restaurant in Seattle that

Peter managed. Even then there was a strong attraction between the two, but there had been no hanky panky. Peter always followed the golden rule of not dipping his pen in the company inkwell. Nevertheless, there was a spark in Seattle.

Nikki's husband was a very wealthy man. He had been the beneficiary of a huge inheritance when his parents died and he had the ego to go along with the size of his bank account. He never had to work and decided to go into politics, which he found to be the perfect career to nurture his immense feeling of self-importance. Fargo had a degree in political science from Yale and became an influential elected official. He was a forceful, persuasive speaker and as his political star rose so did his sky-high opinion of himself. He had become a great leader and political legend in his own mind.

Nikki became tired of lying to constituents for him. Often, when one of his loyal supporters called, he couldn't be bothered to find the time to talk to them on the phone. He made Nikki tell them he was out feeding the chickens. She did it even though they didn't have chickens.

Circumstance put Nikki and Peter together one evening when her husband was out of town on the stump. The spark that started in Seattle was still there and, in the heat of the moment, ignited into a red-hot, romantic fire. Nikki quickly fell out of love with the politician and flamed into love with the hotelier.

Their affair had already lasted eighteen months and was a well-kept secret, or so they thought. The political Fargo traveled a lot, which gave the romantic Fargo plenty of opportunity to be with her lover.

Peter slipped off the couch and locked the door. He returned to his mistress and smoothly removed her clothes as she undressed him. They rubbed and hugged. Before this had all started they had admired each other in public. Now they admired each other in private. She had completely fallen for Peter and he for her. She played him like a song on a clarinet and he moaned to the music until the tune reached its climax.

They embraced a few more moments, and then both realized their time was up and she needed to go back to the others. They quietly dressed and, after one final embrace, she slipped out of the cabin and hurried back down the staircase to the lower deck. The gin game was still in progress and the bailiffs continued to probe for checkmate.

Nikki felt no remorse. After all, she was just an alternate who would play no real role in the trial.

The North Pole was dead ahead.

CHAPTER TWENTY-THREE

KOOTENAI COUNTY COURTHOUSE

Santino had already worked his special kind of black magic by the time the jury returned to the courtroom Monday morning. Nikki Fargo sat in the jury box chair formerly occupied by juror number thirty-nine. Fortunately her mother returned home, perfectly safe, just minutes after Judge Hammond had dismissed thirty-nine from the jury. It was a happy but mysterious ending. The old lady had no idea of where she had been.

"All rise," ordered Jacob, the courtroom bailiff, as the prosecution began its last week of testimony.

CHAPTER TWENTY-FOUR

THE POOL AT THE COEUR d'ALENE INN

Dark blue curtains blocked the view through the glass doors leading to the recreation center at the Coeur d'Alene Inn. A sign posted on the doors read in bold red letters, "Pool area temporarily closed."

"How come the pool is closed?" asked a disappointed pair of youngsters who were spending the night at the Inn while their parents attended a conference at the facility.

General Manager, Wilson Reeburg had relocated his desk to the pool entrance doors to personally stand guard for the duration of the confidential goings-on inside. "Someone broke a glass bottle in the water and we had to drain the pool for safety reasons. We are refilling it now and it should be ready within an hour. Sorry, but we need to put safety first. Tell you what, you two go down to Mulligan's Restaurant near the lobby and I'll ask them to get you boys a couple of big gooey desserts on the house. When you're done with those we ought to be ready for you to swim."

"Oh, great. That's better yet," the oldest boy yelled as the two of them turned around and headed toward the eatery.

Chief Prosecutor James Hart and his team had been staying at the Inn during the Sittinz trial. When he asked a special favor of Reeburg, the G.M. was most happy to comply and tonight was personally protecting his special guest's privacy.

Inside, Hart used the swim ladder to pull himself from the pool after he had finished swimming fifty brisk laps to complete his daily fitness program. It was tough to be away from home so long, but the Inn made a nice home away from home at rates that met the federal per diem.

He dried his hair and face as he walked to the hot tub. It was dark outside but the lighting inside the glass-enclosed recreation area gave the place a warm glow. There was only one other person in the recreation and exercise center. This, of course, was a circumstance which had been carefully preplanned.

She was a lady approximately five feet five inches tall and just slightly overweight, wearing a white swim cap and dark goggles. She sat with her back to the pool and the hotel rooms surrounding it. Hart entered the hot tub and sat opposite the woman.

"The general manager has been very accommodating during our visit. By him helping us to meet this way our conversation will be completely anonymous."

The woman nodded her head but made no sound.

"We will rest our prosecution of this case tomorrow afternoon. The defense seems very confident. Even though you already told us once before you had no indication that any of the jurors were on the take, we felt it would be prudent to have one more conversation with you before we rest and give the defense their opportunity to lie to the jury."

"Since my first report to you, I have continued to go over in my mind everything that was said and done during the time I spent with the jury panel," she replied.

Potential juror number seven, Violet Hemming, had been carefully planted in the panel by the prosecution. It was crucial to the government that the tribunal jury was completely unbiased for this important case. Hemming's role was to be on the lookout for any signs of jury tampering before the trial started.

"There was one juror that seemed to talk more than she should. I think she was a realtor. But, I didn't hear her say anything that would indicate she was trying to sway anybody," recalled Hemming.

"You didn't notice any person trying to make contact with potential jurors around the courthouse or outside during breaks?"

"As I told you before, I watched as closely as I possibly could. I don't know what may have gone on once the jury was empanelled, but during the voir dire there was absolutely nothing suspicious." She sounded slightly annoyed that Hart kept questioning her report, which she had repeated to him on numerous occasions.

"Don't be offended, Violet. I just need to be doggone sure of what we're facing when the defense takes over the trial."

"It's fine. I understand how very important this whole thing is."

"Okay, great," said Hart. "The defense just seems to be acting weird, so I wanted to have one more sit-down with you."

"I hope you've wiped away all the false prostitution and embezzlement charges you conveniently added to my record to tempt any defense efforts to blackmail."

"Oh yes, you have returned to being the outstanding citizen that you have always been. As you said, you can't attest to anything that happened after we used our final preemptory challenge to remove you from the jury panel. But, at least we can have confidence that no games were played before the jury was seated."

"It still seems to me that what we did was a little shady. In a way it was jury tampering in itself, wasn't it?"

"Violet, don't worry. Attorney General Austin himself approved of planting you as a mole on the panel. If you had been seated on the jury there would definitely have been a problem. That's precisely why we saved our final preemptory challenge to take you out of the jury panel at the last possible moment."

"Do you think President Hage knew about Attorney General Austin's approval of this little plot?" she asked.

"General Austin would never admit it and I wouldn't ever dare to ask him. However, if I had to bet my last plug nickel, I'd say the A.G.'s old fraternity brother was in on the plan from the very beginning. They are two peas from the same pod. If any word of this ever leaked out, though, Austin would take the fall." Hart told a fib well, albeit a patriotic fib. He knew darn well from his recent clandestine meeting at the Justice

Building in Washington, D.C., that approval had come from on high.

"Mr. Prosecutor, you can count on my silence. I've been a police officer too long to stop honoring my oath now. Although, being a hooker and a thief for a few weeks was kind of exciting. After all, we all need a little spice in our life even though it was only on paper." The police detective had a big smile on her face as she stepped out of the Jacuzzi, dried and donned her bathrobe.

"Thanks again," yelled the prosecutor. He waved goodbye as Officer Hemming slipped out of the pool area's back door without being seen by anyone. Hart soaked for a few more minutes then stepped out of the hot tub and dried himself. He walked along the side of the blue-tiled pool and headed to the front doors of the recreation center. He pulled back the heavy blue drape that had provided privacy for his secret meeting and opened the door.

Wilson Reeburg was still standing guard. "All done, Mr. Hart?"

"Yep. Thanks a lot. You've been great."

As Hart walked to the room to prepare for his final day of presenting testimony he passed two eager young swimmers with chocolate on their faces racing to the pool. "Yippee, the glass must be all cleaned up 'cause the drapes are open."

They jumped into the big pool feet first, creating an enormous splash that completely soaked the deck.

Hart continued a solitary trek to his room. He stopped in Mulligan's Bar and ordered a Bud Light to go and carried it with him. As he walked down the long hallway toward his guestroom he couldn't understand how the defense could possibly think they had a snowball's chance in hell of winning this case. He and his prosecution team had done a masterful job in exposing the crimes that Sittinz had committed.

Hart reached his room and unlocked the door. He hung his wet towel on a hook in the bathroom, then sat on the end of the bed and twisted the cap off the long-necked bottle and took a drink of the cold beer.

Hart picked up the phone and dialed the room of his senior assistant. "What's the latest on 'Wheels' Payton or whatever in hell they call him?"

"The Ford store phones are clean as a whistle but we still can't figure out that secret number he called. We are making progress, however. It'll just take a little more time."

"Shit," said Hart as he slammed down the phone in an uncharacteristic fit of anger. The pressure was mounting.

How can the defense look so confident?   They either have a bombshell witness or, in some mysterious way, got to a juror after Violet was excused from the panel.   Which was it?

CHAPTER TWENTY-FIVE

KOOTENAI COUNTY COURTHOUSE

Finally, Friday at 3:37 PM the prosecution rested. They had thoroughly proven the guilt of Sittinz beyond the slightest doubt. In absentia, Andrew Bronson, too, was thoroughly implicated as a nom de plume. The prosecution was careful not to allow Bronson the opportunity to go free using a shield of double jeopardy when he was finally brought to trial and, therefore, did not include his name specifically in the complaint pleadings.

The defense knew their client was flattened in court. It was readily apparent on the faces of the jurors. Sittinz's department of defense had virtually nothing to defend with.

Throughout the trial the defense used every legal maneuver they could think of to cry foul. They yelled, "hearsay" thirty-nine times during the proceedings and assailed the objectivity of almost every witness. They attacked the credentials of experts presented by the defense and declared them imposters. Exhibits were besieged as being irrelevant. However, the prosecution withstood every challenge.

"Defense counsel," asked the judge, "are you prepared to begin testimony on Monday morning?"

"Your honor, we are going to need more time to prepare. The prosecution has surprised us with witnesses, testimony, and exhibits that they had not previously shared with us," complained Demerelli in an attempt to stall. He knew very well the harsh reaction his request would generate from the bench. In fact, the instant the words, "more time to prepare," left his mouth he tightened his lips and squinted his eyes to withstand the onslaught he knew was headed his way.

"Defense counsel, please approach the bench," snapped an obviously-upset judge. The gleeful prosecution approached, too. They sauntered to the bench with smirks in anticipation of the verbal whipping that the defense counselors were about to receive.

The three defense lawyers stood below the judge's tall pulpit as though they were little schoolboys about to get a hack from the principal.

"My chambers. Now," was the stern order of the Court.

All rose while his majesty, the judge, stood and left the courtroom. The jury was instructed to wait in the jury room and, as they walked out, the realtor whispered with a snicker to the teacher, "Do you think the judge wears anything under the black robe?"

"Shhh," said the teacher.

The courtroom emptied out quickly as the public hurried to phone, smoke, and gossip.

"Just what testimony and exhibits are you talking about that the prosecution did not inform you of?" questioned Judge Hammond. The veins on his neck stood out and his anger was evident.

"They didn't tell us what questions they were going to ask and we couldn't possibly be expected to anticipate the various angles they explored with the enormous number of witnesses they called," parried Demerelli.

"Oh, really," replied the disbelieving judge. "Maybe the prosecution should get your approval in advance of their line of questioning of each of their witnesses?"

Demerelli didn't really care what opinion the judge had of him and irreverently replied, "Gee, that's a swell idea, your honor. I'm glad you thought of it."

"Counsel, you are about one more smart-ass remark from being held in contempt of court. What is your complaint about the exhibits that were presented?"

"They entered fifty-one exhibits, judge. Don't you think that is a little excessive?"

"Mr. Demerelli, if I had thought they were out of line, don't you think I would have sustained just one of your preposterous objections?"

"Your honor, we need some time to collect our thoughts about the pages of testimony and mountains of exhibits that our opponents have presented. They've spent weeks and weeks laying out their feeble case. It is only fair that we be given time to study all of the testimony they have brought forth, weak as it is," argued Demerelli sensing he needed to back off a little of the attitude he was giving the judge and present some factual basis for his request.

Douglas hung his head in his hands and Stone tightened the muscles of his forehead as he squeezed the bridge of his nose with his thumb and index finger. Douglas peeked out at the judge between his fingers and knew what was coming.

"More time, you say. Very well I will grant you more time. Let's return to the court," ordered the judge.

The jury was reseated in their box and the public hurried back to their pews. Jacob proclaimed the return of Hammond and all rose yet again.

"You sure get your exercise in this guy's court," said the realtor to the teacher in the jury box.

"Shhh," sounded the teacher with her index finger over her lips.

"Be seated," snapped Judge Hammond who was clearly still fuming. "The defense has requested more time to prepare their case. It is now Friday at 4:21 PM. You will not have to return with your case until next Monday at 9 AM sharp!" He hammered the gavel shot one final dig, "If you find yourself a little short of work hours to prepare for Monday you may want to spend a little less time in Whispers at the Resort."

With that he turned and walked through the door leading to his chambers. Of course, all had risen.

CHAPTER TWENTY-SIX

THE COEUR d'ALENE RESORT

The defense was in their Whispers war room. No country-bumpkin judge from Idaho was going to tell them what to do. Anyway, they were just trying to stall for time in the hope that some miracle, like Sittinz having a fatal heart attack, might occur. The tribunal authority that President Hage had conferred on the jury did not allow any appeal so this was the last stand for the defense. They knew they didn't have a leg to stand on and faced worse odds than Custer did at Little Big Horn. The only good thing that had happened so far was that not once did the prosecution have an opportunity to tie Don Vincente Vittori or his organization to Emrae International or Sittinz.

The jury settled into their haven for another long weekend. Even though they were living in the luxury of the Coeur d'Alene, the long weeks were draining and the jurors missed their families and friends. For reasons known only to him, Willie the Ford salesman decided to skip dinner and hide out in his room. The stringent rules were taking a toll on free-spirited "Wheels." Each day saw his mood darken and by now it matched the color of Judge Hammond's black robe. Without his daily sales fix, his depression grew and his wallet shrunk.

The rest assembled in their tightly controlled private dining room. As usual they were eating under the watchful eyes of the bailiffs.

It was Friday night and by now, some of the jurors were ragging on each other. All the glad tidings of the holiday season had given way to bad tidings. The jurors had withdrawn into individual shells and not much was said during the meal. About the only noises were the clink of knives and forks on the ceramic plates and the slurping of soup. About midway through dinner, the lumber mill worker let out a satisfying belch but it didn't attract much attention. He had developed a reputation for burping and farting and the others had simply learned to ignore his irritating habits. He picked his teeth with the tines of his fork.

Nikki Fargo was a fast eater and asked the bailiff for permission to go to the bathroom. The jury was getting tired of having to ask to get approval for everything they did other than sleep.

Nikki entered the middle stall in the ladies' powder room and took a seat. As she held her head in the palms of her hands, she heard a noise. Nikki opened her eyes and looked down to see a large white envelope sliding under the door of the stall. Taped on the outside was a photograph designed to insure that Nikki would open the envelope. She looked down and couldn't believe her eyes.

The picture was of two naked people in the act and showed faces and graphic details. It was a picture of Peter Harding and her. Nikki's heart skipped and she couldn't breathe. She became sick to her stomach and gagged, falling to her knees. Her pantsuit was down around her ankles and she struggled to get her mouth over the toilet bowl. She vomited. Half of it went in the toilet and the other half spewed on her arms, clothes and the floor. She had trouble catching her breath and when she finally did, the rest of her dinner came up. This time she was able to hit the bowl.

She tried desperately to get her wits about her. Tears streamed down her cheeks as she tried to clean her arms and wipe the mess from her clothing. She pulled up her pants and ran to the elevator to go and hide in the privacy of her room.

When Nikki reached her guestroom she threw open the door and jumped under the bedspread in a fetal position. Her eyes were clenched shut and she continued to gag and struggled to breathe. Drops of perspiration beaded on her forehead and the room began spinning. Her entire body was filled with a sickening ache and her head throbbed in pain.

The shrill ring of the phone made her jump. It rang again, then again. Finally, it dawned on her who was calling. She had to answer it. The ringing stopped then started again within seconds. The caller was insistent.

Nikki made herself cough to clear her throat and wiped away the residue of the vomit that remained on her lips with the bed sheet.

"Hello." Nikki tried to make her voice sound normal but it was forced and guttural.

"Nikki, is that you?"

She couldn't talk when she heard the voice. Her mouth opened to acknowledge the caller but no sound came out.

"Nikki, this is Bailiff Foster. Are you all right? When you didn't return to the dinner room, I became worried and checked the bathroom. You weren't there and there was evidence someone had gotten sick. Are you alright?"

Evidence! Damn, did I take the envelope with me when I ran out?

She threw back the blankets on the bed but there was no picture. She tossed the bedspread onto the floor exposing the top sheet. The envelope and picture were there.

"Yes." It was a labored yes, but a word had finally come out of her mouth. "Yes, Betty, I am fine. All of a sudden I became sick to my stomach but I feel fine now. Thank you."

"I can call a doctor or take you to the emergency room if you wish."

"No, that won't be necessary. I'm okay now."

"You're sure?"

"Yes, I am sure, Betty. Thank you for your concern." Of course, Nikki was sure. She was sure she was definitely not okay. "I appreciate your concern for my well being. I'm fine."

"Very well, then I will check on you later."

Nikki hung up the phone and clutched the envelope to her chest. She held it there for several minutes while she summoned the courage to open it. Finally, she did. It had more pictures of the two lovers. They were taken from different angles in the captain's quarters.

Nobody was in there but Peter and me. How and who could have done this?

A smaller envelope was paper clipped to one of the pictures. She opened it with shaking fingers. It was difficult for her to see through the stream of tears pouring from her eyes and she struggled to read the note, which was typed in all lower case letters. It simply read—unlock your balcony door-i will contact you at 7 p.m. sharp–tell nobody about this– and i mean nobody-peter harding.

That was all it said. *What is Peter doing?* Nikki was confused and terribly hurt. She reached for the phone to call the bailiff's control room but stopped short. She looked at her watch. It was 6:29 PM. If she could keep her sanity for a half-hour, maybe she could figure out what was happening to her. She decided it was worth the wait.

Nikki brushed her teeth and gargled with mouthwash to mask the foul barf odor of her breath. She turned on the water in the shower and put her entire head under the hot water to rinse away the sweat and tears but it couldn't wash away the pain and anxiety. Nikki took deep sucking breaths in an effort to regain her composure. After five minutes she stepped out of the shower and dried and cried. She used a hand towel to squeeze the water from her hair then took another and tucked her hair into it forming a turban on top of her head. Nikki looked in the mirror and saw a tired and tear-scarred face.

She was desperate and had trouble focusing on events that were spinning way out of her control. The pictures kept flashing in her mind like a synchronized slide show. Actually seeing the photographs made her realize the terrible risks she had taken. She had given herself, body and mind, to Peter and now he was betraying her, but why?

She put on her bathrobe and walked out of the bathroom into the bedroom. Nikki unlocked the door to the balcony, sat on the end of the bed and waited.

Now what?

CHAPTER TWENTY-SEVEN

THE COEUR d'ALENE RESORT
AND VERONICA WHITCOMB'S LAKE MANSION

Trust, but verify.

Jack Bradley sat at his desk pondering former President Ronald Reagan's famous words describing how the United States should deal with the former Soviet Union's nuclear arsenal treaty promises.

Bradley had the guestroom folios for Douglas, Demerelli and Stone in front of him and was examining them. He had just received titillating information about a surprise strategy the three of them had cooked up but wanted to get a second opinion to verify what he had been told.

He needed to find someone to assist him. A person that had no shame nor cared about the feelings of others, but at the same time was beguiling enough to dig up information without being suspected.

"Christine, please get me Veronica Whitcomb on the phone."

"Absolutely." Christine picked up the phone and dialed the number. Veronica called often to set spa appointments, make dinner reservations, or order limousines. She was not about to go through normal channels to make such arrangements and demanded special treatment. Christine had become her personal concierge and knew Veronica's phone number by heart.

Jack continued to inspect the folios while he waited. They were certainly good customers and it was nice to have the extra business.

"Miss Whitcomb is on line two."

"Veronica, how are you?"

"You know, I'm wonderful."

"I know. Veronica, I need your help."

"Anything for you, Jack Bradley. Well, almost anything."

"I need a little intelligence gathering. I would really like to know how long Douglas and his associates plan to stay at the Resort."

"Jack, how come you're being so cloak-and-dagger? Why don't you just ask them yourself?"

Jack had anticipated the question. "We have a chance to book a very profitable pharmaceutical conference in a couple of weeks, but their meeting planner insists on having the Whitcomb Suite available for their company president to stay in. The planner was so taken with the fine interior decorating job you did, she insists it must be available or she will book at the Broadmoor in Colorado. As you know, Mr. Douglas is using the suite as his headquarters. Well, along with Whispers, of course. He is paying a good rate and I don't want to offend him."

"Jack, what aren't you telling me?"

Trust, but verify, he thought, but didn't say it.

"Seriously, I don't want him to think we're trying to push him out of the suite but, at the same time, I don't want to lose the conference if they'll be gone by then. Plus, this tribunal thing is very touchy. Even asking questions about defense plans or timing might be construed as somehow trying to interfere with the legal process. I thought you could help me without spilling the beans. You can be very persuasive when you want to be."

Bradley's compliment was all it took. "I will be happy to help you. I had a nice conversation with him in the spa and I found him an attractive conversationalist." Even though Veronica did most of the talking in the spa, she was smitten with the handsome Douglas. "I'll invite him to my place tonight."

Whitcomb was a get-it-done person and, just as she promised Jack Bradley, that very same night one of her two bodyguards picked up

Douglas at the Resort and drove him the short distance to Veronica's home on the lake.

The bodyguard turned into a bartender and poured Douglas a stiff Chivas Regal Scotch on the rocks with a twist of lemon. The music of Yanni played throughout the majestic home's sound system and Douglas enjoyed the splendid view of the lake while he listened and drank. Veronica was stylishly late.

After she felt her guest had waited a suitable amount of time for her grand entrance, she stood at the top of the spiral staircase. The bodyguard escorted Douglas from the bar to the living area so the heiress could properly receive him.

Whitcomb was backlit at the top of the staircase. She had specially selected a very thin and revealing white dress. The light from behind silhouetted her body and provided Douglas with a heaping portion of curves and cleavage. She descended the staircase as though she was royalty. In her mind, she was. Cleopatra herself would not have worn finer clothing in either her Egyptian Empire or Roman philandering.

Whitcomb had lined her lair with exquisite enticements. She had the Resort cater a feast of hors d'oeuvres, which she had personally selected.

To begin, Whitcomb plied Douglas with a bottle of Taittinger Collection Lichtenstein Brut Champagne. The scheming hostess knew that the Taittinger spiked by the Chivas would quickly loosen the lawyer's tongue. She planned a roving dinner as they toured her home, which would ensure there would still be time for her to enjoy her special dessert of musclemen later in the evening. At strategic locations along the tour path she had placed such delicacies as salmon mousse croustades, shrimp bouchee, and lobster medallions with Beluga caviar.

Douglas was particularly excited when they encountered fresh-shucked oysters on the half shell in the master bedroom. It was a clear indication that Veronica had some real treats in store for him after the tour. She was cunning; the oysters were just a delicate tease she threw in for the tickle.

The tour of her palace culminated in her extraordinary tiled seven-car garage, which housed three cars. A blue four-wheel drive Lincoln

Navigator for winter driving was in the middle. On one side of the SUV was a collector's classic green Austin Healy and on the other side, a brand new fiery red Thunderbird.

The other four spots were filled with boats, very special and beautiful wooden boats.

"Coeur d'Alene is becoming the wooden boat capital of the west and I am developing my own stable of classics. Every summer there is a wonderful wooden boat show along the floating boardwalk surrounding the Resort."

Douglas was smashed but admired the collection through his fog. "They're damn petty, I mean pretty," he stumbled. He couldn't get his mind off the oysters in the master bedroom.

Motivated by her Pharaonic narcissism, Veronica teased her guest deliciously with her supple body. She allowed him little sneak peaks as she bent down low, then reached high, to show him various parts of her boats and herself. "Do you like my stern and keel? These woody boats are very exciting, don't you think?"

In spite of his drunken stupor he was starting to get a woody of his own.

The exquisite hostess had the brains to use her body to get Douglas to talk. "Let me share with you my newest little micro-yacht. This little beauty has a deep V hull." She waved her arms to show off the hull and made sure the top of her dress opened just enough to be a part of the show as well. "It's designed after one of the Chesapeake Bay oyster boats of the 1920s."

Another reference to oysters, he thought. *She's trying to tell me something. This is going to be great.*

"You know, they used to tong oysters with these," she teased.

Oh, baby!

Whitcomb caressed the boat with her perfectly manicured fingernails. "This little yacht has a plumb stem and a torpedo stern with a long narrow length to width ratio!" She exaggerated each word to emphasize its possible double entendre.

Douglas was about ready to explode and made a pass at her. He grabbed her around the waist and she made a quick two-step. "You don't have to talk about oysters or keels or stems anymore, Veronica. I'm ready right now," he exclaimed. She had him to the point where he was putty in her hands. If he knew the firing codes to the nation's nuclear arsenal, she could get him to tell her now.

"Wonderful, but not tonight. How about getting together in a week or so to finish our excursion?"

"We need to bring our little tour to a climax now because I'll be gone within just a few days, if not sooner."

Veronica had the information she needed for General Manager Jack Bradley.

"Come on," he urged. "This is a perfect time to horse around."

"Sorry," said Veronica firmly. She looked toward her two brawny bodyguards who were hiding around the corner just in case their queen needed help. "I've got my own horses to attend to tonight. One's a thoroughbred I use when I like to go fast and the other is a stallion. Sometimes I ride them both in the same night."

Just like that, Douglas was in the back seat of the Navigator and whisked back to his room at the Resort. The inebriated lawyer was confused and wasn't sure what had just happened. All he knew was that, as he lay on his back atop the bedspread, the ceiling and walls were spinning wildly.

While Veronica waited for her guards to return to watch over her body, she picked up the phone and gave Bradley the news she had scammed out of Douglas.

"Thank you, Veronica. Well done," complimented Jack. He flash hooked the phone to clear the line without replacing the handset. Three seconds later, he was dialing to report and verify.

The bodyguards returned and were told it was time for the imperial hot bath. The two stripped naked and sat in the hot tub.

Cleopatra walked down the steps into the Jacuzzi fully clothed and took her place between her two Roman Centurions. Her thin dress clung tightly to her body clearly accentuating all of her special parts. The Imperial Guards carefully removed her royal robes, battle spears hardened and ready. Caesar and Mark Anthony be damned. The Egyptian Queen had her own personal Centurions in the heart of her castle in Rome d'Alene.

CHAPTER TWENTY-EIGHT

THE COEUR d'ALENE RESORT AND KOOTENAI COUNTY COURTHOUSE

The knock on her room door startled Nikki. She was expecting contact from the balcony. She went to the door and looked through the peephole. Nobody was in sight.

"Peter?" she called. "Peter are you there?"

Nothing. Nikki opened the door a crack and looked out. Still nothing. She stepped out into the hallway and looked both ways. The hallway was vacant. She went back into her room and closed the door. She latched the security deadbolt and rested her head against the inside of the door.

What in the world is happening to me?

She turned to go back to the bed and as she did, a man dressed in dark clothes reached out to grab her. She started to scream but, before a sound could leave her lips, a hairy hand slapped over her mouth.

"Shut up. Do not make a peep or you will never speak again," he threatened. He squeezed her face and dug in hard with his thumb and fingers as he shook her head. "Do you understand?"

Nikki, eyes wide open and filled with tears, shook her head up and down.

He placed the business end of a long sharp knife on her throat, "I am going to take my hand from your mouth. Keep it shut." She did. He threw her on the bed and kept the knife pointed directly at her face. It was not Peter.

Santino looked like a dumb Sicilian, but in fact, he was a very smart one. At least as smart as a maniacal, ruthless butcher can be. His original plan was to rent a room above Nikki's and rappel down from that balcony to hers. However, as he cased the Resort he discovered something that even long-time employees of the hotel didn't know. A very sophisticated camera monitoring system had been secretly located deep in the bowels of the hotel when it was first built. Almost all of the exterior and grounds were monitored, as were the public spaces inside. Only General Manager Jack Bradley and a handful of trusted employees knew of its existence and location. Surveillance was a stealthy operation, separate even from the security department. Eighty-one televisions, nine high and nine wide, were lined up on a wall in the surveillance room. It was a system that would have made Caesar's Palace in Las Vegas proud.

When the Resort was first built, rumors circulated by workmen who noticed extra wiring being installed in the building that the place was being built in anticipation of gambling coming to Idaho. The rumors were so persistent that bets were made in town as to how many years it would be before slot machines were installed. It was simply not true. The mysterious electrical work was for the cameras.

Santino had to come up with a cunning new plan. He observed that when the jury went to dinner each night, the Resort housekeeping department provided turn-down service to freshen up the room. While they performed this service they left the guestroom door propped open. This night, when housekeeping entered the room, Santino, wearing a stolen houseman's uniform over his own clothes, placed a plastic stopper in the door lock to prevent the latch from completely closing. When the housekeeping staff left, he pushed the door open, entered the room and hid under the bed. The balcony story was just a ploy. His cohort's knock on the door was designed to give Santino time to come out from under the bed and surprise Nikki.

Now his mission was to scare the living hell out of her and threaten exposure of her passionate affair with Harding. "You have seen the pictures. We have many more. If we release them to the media, your life will be ruined, not to mention your husband's political career. You won't be able to show your face anywhere."

Santino and his gang had been given the responsibility to find dirt on any possible member of the jury. Dirt was an area of great expertise for them and they cleverly uncovered the affair between Fargo and Harding. Santino's spies learned of the jury's cruise in advance and he had a hunch that this might be an opportunity for Nikki and Harding to make contact. He was right.

Santino duped a deck hand into letting him take a self-guided tour of the vessel under the guise that he was considering a wedding cruise for his daughter. When he reached the top deck, he concealed a set of hidden motion-activated cameras in each of the four corners of the captain's quarters. The full color still photographs lifted from the tapes now proved to be useful tools for blackmail.

"What . . . what do you want? Where is Peter?"

"Harding knows nothing about this. I typed the note."

"Who are you? How did you get in here?"

"None of your business. You will do exactly as I tell you. If you go to the judge, both you and Harding will be killed." Santino's voice was bloodcurdling.

"What does the judge have to do with this?" She sobbed, as tears streamed from her swollen eyes.

"Sittinz is innocent. The government has set him up with planted evidence and has him dangling like a worm on a fishhook. We need to be sure he receives justice by being set free. You must vote to acquit him of these false charges."

"I can't do that."

"Then you will suffer the consequences and they will be horrific. Look at these pictures," he said as he threw them at her.

"I'm only one vote anyway. You'll never get the rest of them. You can't possibly think I can convince eleven other people even if I did go along with you."

"A guilty verdict in this case must be unanimous. One vote, your vote, can set an innocent man free. You will vote not guilty. Do you understand?" Santino held the sharp knife close to her left eye and twisted it in his hand slightly to make sure she knew he meant business.

Nikki was scared to death and her body trembled. He left her no choice. She squeezed her eyes shut and quietly whispered, "Yes."

Court convened promptly at 9 AM Monday morning. By now, the jury and public had been so conditioned that, like Pavlov's dog, they were already standing when Judge Hammond entered the room and did so even before the courtroom bailiff was able to announce the justice's imperial entrance.

"Be seated," said the judge without looking up. He pounded his gavel harder than normal to let the defense know he was still steamed at them for their attempted delay tactics. "Defense counsel, are you ready to proceed?"

"Yes, your honor, we are," responded Douglas. He stood to address the jury and for nearly three minutes paced back and forth in front of them looking each of them directly in the eyes. Finally he began to speak in a clear firm voice, "The prosecution has totally failed to produce one shred of evidence that would lead to the conviction of my client of any crime. We ask your honor to declare a directed verdict and end this outlandish charade now."

"Denied," declared Judge Hammond without even looking up from his desk. He picked up a bundle of papers but was squinting as he struggled to read them. "Let me ask you counselor, how many of these, these. . . ?" The judge fumbled for his glasses, "Oh, yes here they are. How many of these one hundred and twenty-one names on your potential witness list do you plan to call during your defense portion of the case?"

The defense attorneys had instructed their secretary to type the names on their potential witness list in the smallest type possible because they knew the judge's eyesight was fading. They enjoyed every little thing they could possibly do to get his goat. After all, they had utterly no need for the judge's good will.

"Your honor, I need a few moments to confer with my client and associates," said Douglas.

The judge was further annoyed with yet another delay needed for

Douglas to answer even the simplest of questions.

"Fine," hollered the judge as he rocked back in his chair and threw his reading glasses across the bench in disgust.

I imagine these big city lawyers will call each and every one of these hundred and twenty-one witnesses if for no other reason than to justify their inflated fees. I bet we're going to be here for another three months.

Douglas didn't need to confer with his team but turned as though he was going to talk to them anyway. He didn't speak but, with his back to the bench, just put his hands on the table, leaned forward toward his associates and smiled broadly. No backwoods judge was going to pull the wool over his eyes. He turned back and stared one more time at Nikki Fargo. She returned the look then cast her eyes downward signaling shameful acquiescence. Douglas stood tall, looked directly at the judge and confidently proclaimed, "Your honor, the defense rests."

The judge was astounded and leaned forward in his chair as he said loudly, "What did you say?"

Douglas repeated slowly mouthing each word, "Your–honor–the–defense—rests!"

Judge Hammond couldn't believe his ears. He rubbed his forehead and temples while trying to comprehend the implications of the defense's startling bolt from the blue. "Approach the bench."

The entire battery of barristers, from both sides, stood before the high perch in which the judge nested. "Do you understand what you are doing?"

"Yes, we do your honor," replied Douglas speaking flatly.

"You fully realize that, given the Presidential Tribunal Order under which this case is being heard, there is no appeal from the jury's decision of verdict or sentencing?" The judge realized he had jumped to a conclusion that the verdict would be guilty. He cleared his throat and quickly added, "That is, if a sentence is necessary."

"Thank you, your honor, for at least giving us the benefit of the doubt that our client just might be innocent," said Demerelli.

Each defense attorney answered in the affirmative when the judge polled them to be sure there was unanimous consent. Their smug smiles unnerved Hammond.

The judge looked at the prosecutors to see if they had anything at all to say. They didn't. They too, were entirely bewildered by the remarkable turn of events.

"Very well. Mr. Curtis Sittinz, please stand." The accused man meekly obeyed the judge's command. "Mr. Sittinz, do you understand what your counsel is doing here?"

"Yes, your honor."

The puzzled judge continued, "Mr. Douglas, the rules of the tribunal order say you can decide how much time you need before you and the prosecution present your jury instructions as long as I consider your request reasonable. I certainly understand you may well need several days to prepare your briefs and the Court is prepared to be generous in this regard. How much time do you want?"

"Your honor we are ready at this very moment."

"Mr. Douglas, did you say you are ready now?"

"Yes, sir."

In all his years, the judge had never experienced anything like this. He waved both hands signaling the two sides to step forward with their jury instructions. The defense placed one small envelope on the bench. The prosecution passed out the thirty-one instructions they had completed to date. Judge Hammond read over the prosecutor's numerous pages then opened the envelope, which had been presented by the other side. It had one sheet of paper in it. Hammond looked at one side and then the other. It was blank. The defense was not offering one single instruction to help guide the jury to their way of thinking.

Judge Hammond was incredulous. All he could do as the mediator was to proceed. He read the thirty-one instructions to the jury and briefed them on the procedures the jurors should use during their deliberations. The defense team smiled as though they were cats that had just swallowed the mice. Douglas looked at Nikki and winked. Finally, the judge gave the case to the jury. "Ladies and gentlemen of the jury, this case is now yours to decide. You may now, once and for all, finally discuss this case amongst yourselves."

As the jury filed out of the courtroom the teacher said to the realtor, "Yes, I think Sittinz is kind of cute. I think the judge wears normal clothes under his robe, although it would be fun to look, and both of us need the exercise."

"Oh," said the ditsy realtor.

CHAPTER TWENTY-NINE

COEUR d'ALENE

"Did you see the look on the face of that son-of-a-bitchin' judge? I thought the old fart was gonna have a heart attack," roared Stone.

"I loved it. His honor, the hillbilly seemed a little confused," chided Demerelli. "I think the old gas bag finally realizes he's a little out of his league."

"No question, his elevator doesn't quite run all the way to the top floor," said Douglas.

Stone, Demerelli and Douglas were completely filled with contempt for the court.

The attorneys for the defense were celebrating their brilliant courtroom strategy with lunch and libations in their favorite watering hole, Whispers. They toasted their shrewdness and superb courtroom tactics. They had renamed their war room the victory garden!

Soon, they would be flying home first class and their client would go Scot-free. They did have a few anxious moments but, as expected, they would be leaving the courtroom triumphantly. They had drawn victory from the jaws of certain defeat and were sure to receive huge bonuses from their benefactor. Things could not have worked out better. The sweet smell of success filled the air.

"Mr. Douglas, you have a telephone call," announced Jack Bradley's secretary, Christine. The call for the defense attorneys was originally routed to her and she had a very good idea just where they might be. "You can take it here at the bar or I would be happy to transfer it to a private office for you."

"Thank you kindly, but the phone at the bar will be just fine, young lady. I appreciate your help," said the smiling Douglas. He stood and was whistling as he swaggered to the bar while his partners continued the celebration. Times were good.

Douglas returned in less than a minute. He was sullen and ashen-faced. "What the hell's the matter with you?" Stone asked.

"That was the courtroom bailiff on the phone. He told me the jury is coming back in."

"What? That's impossible," said Stone. "They've been in the jury room for less than three hours."

"Let's go, men," ordered Douglas.

The now-worried threesome hustled to the courthouse. The building was just three blocks from the Resort so they were there within five minutes. When they arrived they went directly to the bailiff. "What's going on?" demanded Douglas.

"The jury has a question they need to have answered before they can begin serious deliberations. Court will resume in a few minutes."

"Oh," sighed Douglas with relief. The defense team's confidence began to return and color began to come back in Douglas's face. It was not unusual at all for the jury to be somewhat confused at the beginning of their discussions, especially in a case like this with the tribunal implications and uncertainties.

Everything is okay after all. They just have a procedural question. I'll bet they haven't even selected a foreman yet.

The defense attorneys had their backs to the jury box as the jury itself re-entered the courtroom. Douglas, Demerelli and Stone were explaining to their client just what was going on and reassuring him that this was a normal circumstance. They comforted him with the knowledge that he should not be overly concerned.

"I understand you, the members of the jury, have a question for the Court," stated Judge Hammond who was again seated at the bench.

Juror number thirty-two stood. He was the part-time cruise boat captain who had immigrated to America from Norway twenty-five years ago. He still spoke with a heavy accent, "Your honorable honor, I have been selected as the jury foreman and ve do have a question for you, sir." His hands were noticeably shaking. He held a piece of white paper upon which he had written some notes. The foreman wanted to be sure he was accurate in addressing his question to the judge. His shaking hands seemed to give the piece of paper a life of its own. It bobbled from side to side as though it was made of Jell-O.

"Very well. Go right ahead and ask," guided the judge.

The defense, prosecution, and public all had their eyes glued on the foreman. The man spoke slowly and deliberately, "Ve understand dat ve are to decide a verdict and set a sentence. Ve furder understand dat ve are to make both decisions and present them to you at the same time ven ve return to the courtroom following our discussions."

"That is correct. Of course, if the verdict is not guilty there will be no sentencing," confirmed Judge Hammond. He had remembered his earlier guffaw and was careful not to repeat it.

The foreman continued, "Yes ve understand dat. If ve do set a sentence can dis sentencing be for life vitout pardon ever being a possibility?"

The defense sat straight up in their chairs. They were stunned and befuddled. Douglas looked toward Nikki's chair to get some eye or head movement to explain what the heck was happening. She wasn't in the chair! He scanned the entire jury box. Nikki Fargo was not there. In her chair sat the second alternate.

What the hell? What's going on? thought Douglas.

"Yes, you can impose a sentence of life imprisonment without the possibility of parole," said his honor. "Do you or any other member of the jury have any other questions?"

"No, sir," responded the foreman as he took his seat in the jury box.

"Fine," said the judge. "The Court does have one other announcement regarding juror sixty-three." That was the number of Nikki Fargo but the judge did not announce her name publicly. "Juror number sixty-three has been transported to Kootenai Medical Center where she is in the intensive care unit. Juror number ninety-eight, the second alternate who sat through the entire trial, will be taking that particular seat." Hammond gave no further details regarding Nikki's illness. He gaveled the session to a close. The jury retired to do their duty.

The prosecution and the public vacated the courtroom while the defense team and their client Curtis Sittinz sat dumbfounded staring at the empty bench and jury box. Not one of them said a word for several minutes. Douglas looked at the vacant chair that was supposed to be occupied by their special juror, Nikki Fargo. Demerelli gazed blankly at the portrait of President Hage that hung on the courthouse wall and Stone fingered the pile of legal briefs lying on the table in front of him. Sittinz kept looking back and forth from one defender to the other in hopes that one of them would be considerate enough to tell him what in the hell had just happened to him.

These same three lawyers had assured him just a few minutes earlier that there was nothing to worry about and this entire unfortunate misunderstanding would take care of itself in no time. They even suggested he begin to get his belongings together because he would be leaving custody and returning to freedom in the very near future. They seemed supremely confident that total victory was just around the corner.

"It ain't over till it's over," said Demerelli breaking the silence. "We've still got a card or two to play. Remember, it takes a unanimous vote of the jury to convict even if eleven of 'em want to hang you."

Sittinz rubbed his neck and sat silently looking at the ceiling.

Nikki Fargo was taken to the hospital, but in perfect health under the protective custody of the Federal Bureau of Investigation.

Nikki was able to compose herself after Santino left her room. Even though it was against the rules, a back channel of communication allowed her to contact Peter Harding during her incarceration as a member of the jury.

Jurors were allowed to have room service and Peter had rigged a special tray with a hollow center that allowed them to send each other secret love notes. The bailiffs checked the trays before delivery but did not think to look underneath. She contacted Peter and let him know she desperately needed to talk to him.

Nikki told Peter she had promised her blackmailer a vote to acquit Sittinz but simply could not bring herself to do such a thing. They knew they had to confess to their affair. Justice in the Emrae International scandal was much more important than the sanctity of their personal lives, no matter how difficult it would be to admit the truth.

Peter met with Jack Bradley and together they developed a plan to shield Peter and Nikki from harm and, at the same time, set a trap.

Bradley convinced Judge Hammond, the prosecution, and the FBI that events had created a fascinating opportunity. Rather than punish Nikki and Peter they could benefit from their co-operation.

Santino had been careful when he entered Nikki's room, but not careful enough. Bradley's surveillance monitors caught him on film. The picture was dark and grainy but clear enough for Nikki to confirm it was the blackmailer. The FBI was well aware of Santino and knew for whom he worked. The possibilities of widening their net grew exponentially. Santino's connection served as confirmation of the involvement of the Vittori Crime Family in the Emrae scandal.

By giving immunity to Nikki in exchange for her help there was a good chance they could snare Sittinz, Santino and just maybe Vincente Vittori. Nikki's affair would remain secret. By taking her to the hospital, the alibi that she had been removed from the deliberations due to illness was corroborated.

A decision was made to keep Nikki on the jury until the defense rested. The judge had been given assurance the defense would rest early. The FBI had their sources. The plan worked perfectly.

CHAPTER THIRTY

THE MANSION OF VINCENTE VITTORI
BUFFALO, NEW YORK AND COEUR d'ALENE

Anthony Cordero arrived at the estate of Vincente Vittori to personally deliver the bad news that the Sittinz case was not going well, just as he had done when the feds nabbed Sittinz in Tropican. This time Santino was not around. He was late returning from his mission to intimidate Nikki Fargo and there was concern as to his whereabouts.

The Don entered the library. "How can such a thing happen, Antonio? You had told me there was little hope of Sittinz going free unless we made special arrangements. Now they have fallen apart. Sittinz is weak and they will break him."

"Yes, I know Don Vittori."

"And these attorneys. How is it that they present no defense? Not even one witness," complained the Don in a strained, upset voice.

"I had no idea they were planning such an ill-advised move. That was their strategy and I had absolutely no involvement in that decision. They do think that there is still a possibility Sittinz will go free."

Don Vittori paced back and forth across the room. He rubbed his forehead and brushed his fingers through his thinning hair. Sittinz's pathetic weakness, the bungling defense attorneys, and the fact that Santino was AWOL were all very troubling.

"We can't gamble on the opinion of the defense attorneys. Any chance for Sittinz to be convicted must be eliminated," announced Vittori after he had carefully considered the situation. Cordero was unsettled.

The mansion's butler stood in the doorway and said, "Santino just came through the main gate. He stopped in Chicago on his way home and shacked up with an old girlfriend for a couple of nights. He'll be here in a moment."

At least the Don had one less worry now that Santino had returned. "Send him right in. Get him some espresso."

With the arrival of Santino, the Italian version of the Afghan loya jirga was now complete and they hatched an intricate plan to eliminate any possibility of Sittinz facing conviction.

Santino was dispatched back to Coeur d'Alene immediately along with two Vitorri family soldiers. The Don made sure the flight didn't connect through Chicago.

The plan to spring Sittinz had to unfold quickly. Once the jury came in with a verdict it would be nearly impossible to get to him. But, Santino was extremely good at his job and had learned long ago that careful planning was the key to success in his criminal profession.

During his previous trip, Santino had noticed a remarkable resemblance between one of the bailiffs working the case and Curtis Sittinz. The major difference was hair color, but a carefully selected hat could solve that problem. Sittinz was five feet eleven inches tall and the bailiff was six foot one. This little challenge could be handled by remodeling a pair of shoes resembling those the bailiff wore. An additional inch of heel and sole would get Sittinz very close to the height of the taller bailiff. Adding any more than an inch could make the defendant unsteady on his feet. A uniform and badge exactly matching that of the bailiff would complete the disguise.

At the Kootenai County Jail, Douglas briefed Sittinz during their daily morning meeting. "Tonight at 5:30 PM we have arranged to have you brought before the judge because you want to have a little talk and negotiate with him. We have hinted you have some interesting information you want to share and you'll meet only with him and nobody else. In fact, you don't even want us in there with you. They won't leave you completely alone with him but they'll allow you to meet with just one bailiff present so you will feel free to sing.

"The almighty judge is already drooling. I imagine he's thinking of himself as a heroic small town judge who wiggles a confession out of the century's biggest swindler."

"Shit. I'm not thrilled with you calling me the century's biggest swindler," objected Sittinz.

"Oh, of course, forgive me. I'm sorry. Anyway if our luck holds, the taller one of the bailiffs will escort you into the judge's chambers for your little one-on-one chat. He's his honor's personal bailiff so we're pretty confident he'll be the one. Just to make sure, Demerelli and Stone will keep the other bailiffs busy by asking them a bunch of dumb questions."

"What kind of questions?"

"Busy work questions to keep them tied up and away from the judge's chambers. Just exactly what will happen in the courtroom after the jury comes in? You know, shit like how much time will we have with you when the guilty verdict is announced?"

"Jesus, can't you give me a glimmer of hope the verdict might be not guilty?"

"Oh, sorry again, be we won't have to wait and see about that little detail, anyway. The Buffalo crowd is going to spring you and get you back to Tropican and your little harem in no time. You make small talk and mealy mouth for exactly twelve minutes, and then say you've changed your mind and tell the judge to stick it."

"Are you sure about this?"

"All I can tell you is what I've been instructed to tell you from the people in Buffalo. When the bailiff escorts you out of the judge's chamber and into the receptionist's room, he'll shut the door to the judge's office. Hammond's phone will ring and tie him up at his desk for at least a two-minute nonsense call to make sure he doesn't come out. At that moment, both doors will be shut and you and the bailiff will be isolated in the outer office that leads to the courtroom. The bailiff will be sprayed with a temporary sleeping gas by two goons hiding in the closet. They will stuff the bailiff into the same closet they jumped out of and he'll doze for twenty minutes or so, and then wake up just fine."

"Just how are they gonna get into the closet unnoticed?"

"That's another reason my two associates are going to be having their little talk with the other bailiffs. They'll have them tied up in a heated conversation, which will allow enough time for your two helpers to sneak into the judge's outer office. After they subdue your guard they'll help you put on a bailiff costume including a cute little wide brimmed hat we got you and some special shoes to make you look a little taller. They appear to be lace up shoes but that part's fake. They Velcro shut for quick assembly."

"Santino thinks of everything," Sittinz said admiringly. He had met Santino several times at Don Vittori's estate and Sittinz was always impressed by the Sicilian's ability to organize crime.

I wonder what old Andy is up to, thought Sittinz after Bronson came to mind, *probably boffing some babe's lights out on the French Riviera.*

"I hear the big boss himself played a hand in this caper. You're obviously damn important to him. Walk right out the door and straight through the very courtroom they're trying to roast you in. Santino will hustle you down to the Coeur d'Alene Resort."

"Why don't we just split and run then," asked Sittinz.

"Because the cops will have the roads shut down in no time. I'm told they're gonna supply you with a change of clothes and rush you to a helicopter waiting to take off at the Resort's helipad. If we land it anywhere else it'll draw suspicion. The Resort's got choppers coming in and out of the place regularly so it won't be anything out of the ordinary there. Then, the plan is to smuggle you aboard a chartered jet to Tropican. This time they will make damn sure you're provided suitable security. Hell, they may even want to give your ugly mug a facelift to make you a little more invisible. Questions?"

"Nope, I got it." He was surprisingly composed.

"Kind of a remarkable twist of fate," said Douglas.

"What's that?"

"There's quite a little irony in this plan. For a few minutes, while you're in the bailiff's uniform at the Resort, you'll be guarding your own jury."

CHAPTER THIRTY-ONE

KOOTENAI COUNTY COURTHOUSE AND
THE COEUR d'ALENE RESORT

Indeed, Sittinz's look-alike guard escorted him into the judge's chamber at exactly 5:30 PM. The judge sat expectantly behind his desk wearing his black robe. A starched white shirt collar and the knot of a bright red tie poked out of the robe at the neckline. His elbows were resting on the desk with the fingers of his two hands intertwined. As the prisoner entered, the judge spread his fingers apart and with the open palm of his right hand, invited Sittinz to sit in his presence.

"You have requested this meeting," said the judge.

"Yes, I did." He stopped at that point, seeming to make the judge beg for more information.

Hammond was too excited to let a little irritation ruin his moment in the sun. He could see the mouse nibbling at the cheese he had placed in his judicial trap. "Please continue."

"Yes, your honor," the prisoner slowly said, "you are correct. I did call for this meeting. I hoped it could be private because I have something very important to share with you."

The judge's heart pounded faster in anticipation. "Mr. Sittinz," said

Hammond as calmly as possible so as not to spook his little cheese-nibbler, "it is rare that I would meet with a defendant even with his counsel and the prosecution in the room. I have agreed to meet with you and have excluded all of them. My bailiff is the only person in the room other than you and me. Surely, you must feel comfortable with this arrangement?"

"Could I have some water?" asked Sittinz.

"Water?"

"Yes sir, my mouth is very dry. This whole discussion is very difficult for me."

The judge gave a nod of approval to the bailiff who poured ice water from the judge's silver-plated water pitcher into a plastic cup.

"Thank you," said the mouse. He took a long slow swig of the water, held it in his mouth a long time, and then swallowed.

Four minutes had gone by. Sittinz nervously kept looking at his watch. "You know, your honor, there are some people out there that think I may be found guilty."

No shit, thought the judge but didn't speak. He slowly shook his head up and down indicating that such a possibility certainly existed. He waited for the mouse to continue.

"Well," Sittinz said speaking slowly, "it's possible they're right." The defendant took another drink from the cup and this time drained it. He looked at the bailiff and raised the cup requesting a refill.

The bailiff looked at the judge for permission to serve more water. The judge was hesitant about further delay. He looked back at Sittinz and, remembering his objective, flashed a smile. "Go ahead, bailiff. I'm sure this whole matter is quite an ordeal for our friend here."

The bailiff handed the refilled cup to their new friend and Sittinz took another deliberate, long, slow drink.

"And you've come to tell me something?" It took all of Hammond's composure to stay seated on his chair. He was about ready to leap up in the jubilation of his upcoming fifteen minutes of fame.

"Well, yes. If I were to, well, if I were to give you some information I think could be important for you to know, I mean, would that be a good thing for me to do?" He looked at his watch again. Nine minutes had elapsed.

"Well of course, son," praised the judge in a grandfatherly way as he rubbed hi s hands together in anticipation. "I would certainly be glad to hear information you feel would be helpful in the administration of justice." He set a little more bait. "We're interested in finding a fair solution for *all* involved."

One minute to go.

"Well judge, I hope someday you thank me for this and I appreciate your taking me into your confidence."

The judge was about ready to explode, "Yes?"

Time was up. "Your honor, I think you should take your gavel and stick it right straight up your fat ass!"

"What the..." screamed the judge as he stopped himself mid-sentence. He realized he'd been had. He stood flailing both arms wildly in the air and motioning to the bailiff, "Get this no-good son-of-a bitch out of my office! Now!"

The bailiff jumped into action and grabbed the prisoner by the scruff of his neck and pulled him out the inner office door. The judge's phone rang just as the door shut.

The plan was working to perfection. The bailiff was out like a light. The two thugs, who had posed as termite exterminators to gain access to the courthouse, helped Sittinz dress. The bailiff's badge had already been pinned to the shirt. He slipped the shoes on his feet and Velcro'd the fake laces shut. He was ready to go. He pulled the wide-brimmed hat down on his head as he quickly walked through the courtroom while the goons put the real bailiff to bed in the closet. The escaper stumbled a bit in the awkward shoes.

Santino was in position and pushed Sittinz into the back of the van he had waiting outside. He drove at exactly the legal speed limit to the Coeur d'Alene Resort just three blocks away. They entered, in the sight of God and all, right through the chrome revolving front doors of the Resort. Several members of the staff recognized Sittinz as the bailiff he wasn't, and said hi.

Jack Bradley personally sat in front of his sophisticated monitoring system and was in constant radio contact with the FBI. "They just entered the front door," Bradley announced over the radio.

"Check," responded the FBI agent handling the channels between the Resort and the agents on site. "Everyone is in place."

"They've just entered the elevator," alerted Bradley. "They will be at the elevator landing on the eighteenth floor in 17 seconds and to the suite ten seconds after that."

"Copy," said the agent.

Santino pushed the elevator button. He held the keycard to his suite in one hand. His other hand was in his pocket fingering his lethal switchblade knife. "The helicopter is already warming up on the Resort's helipad," lied Santino. The helipad was, in fact, quiet and empty. Don Vincente Vittori was one who took no chances. He had lost all confidence in the defense attorneys and felt Sittinz was certain to be convicted. The Don decided to carry out the ultimate sentence in advance of the verdict just to be prudent. He always erred on the side of prudence.

The Juniper Suite was one of three located on top of the Resort's eighteen-story tower overlooking the lake. The suite was spacious inside and also had two large tiled balconies; one of which would become the fatal platform used to carry out Don Vittori's death sentence.

The knife would only be used as a tool to coax Sittinz off the balcony and fall to his certain death. It was dark outside and nobody would even know from what room he had jumped. It would appear Sittinz escaped so he could commit suicide on his own terms. A note in a room on the seventeenth floor would tell of his desire to finally escape the horrors of prison and set himself free by taking his own life. Authorities wouldn't buy the story but it would complicate things for their investigation and create some further doubt about what really happened. The most important part of the plan was that no trail could possibly lead to Vittori after Sittinz had been executed.

Santino told Sittinz to change clothes, including his shoes. The escaper was ready in two minutes and brushed his hair back with his fingers. Santino would dispose of the clothing when he returned. "Follow me, we're gonna take a short cut to the helipad on the roof." The real helipad was located atop another wing of the Resort but Sittinz had no idea. He had never been to the Resort. The only place he'd vacationed in Coeur d' Alene was the Crossbar Hotel. Santino had placed a tall ladder on the corner balcony of the Suite. "Okay, Sittinz, hop up the ladder. I'll be right behind you. We'll be out of here in no time." The assassin held his knife in his left hand out of view from Sittinz.

"I don't hear the helicopter," said Sittinz as he put his foot on the first step and grabbed the ladder with both hands.

"You will in a moment. Hurry."

Sittinz was half way up the ladder. Santino was right behind him and looked down to the ground far below. He had duped his victim exactly as planned and the time was ripe to send him to his death. *Don Vittori will be proud of me.* Santino snapped open his switchblade and grabbed Sittinz's right leg.

"Stop right there. FBI, you're under arrest," hollered an FBI agent looking down from the roof, gun in hand.

Both criminals' eyes looked up searching the darkness for the voice. A powerful flashlight beam momentarily blinded both of them and six agents charged out on the balcony.

"Drop the knife, Santino," screamed an agent as she ran through the balcony doorway.

Santino let the knife fall to the balcony floor. "How the hell? Where did you guys come from?"

The agents cuffed both men, read them their rights and hauled both of them down the elevator and out the front doors of the Resort. Three unmarked FBI cars, flanked by Kootenai County Sheriff's cruisers, were stationed under the porte-cochere. The first held the two goons that had been picked up at the courthouse still wearing their fake exterminators' uniforms. The second awaited Santino and the third was for Sittinz who would remain in Coeur d'Alene to face the jury he had guarded a few minutes earlier.

My plan was so carefully concocted, thought Santino as the FBI Agents pushed his head down and forced him to enter the back seat of the sheriff's car. Not once, did he have the slightest inkling that his plot would be thwarted. *How could they possibly have known?*

CHAPTER THIRTY-TWO

BUFFALO AND COEUR d'ALENE

Precisely two minutes after the sheriff's cruisers carrying Santino, Sittinz, and the other two gangsters had raced out from under the Resort's porte-cochere, three teams of FBI agents sprung into action on opposite sides of the country.

In Buffalo, two white municipal utility vans were parked outside the mansion of Vincente Vittori. He was in the library talking on the phone. The FBI agents inside the vans knew this because they had a high-powered directional listening device pointed directly at the middle of the large stained glass window. They heard every word as if they were sitting next to him.

It was already well into the night, Eastern Standard Time. The Don was nervously sitting in his favorite chair in the library. He fidgeted and fingered the stem of his wine glass as he anxiously awaited a call on his scramble phone from Santino confirming, in code of course, that the dirty deed had been done.

The agents were not listening to anything important. Vittori was talking to one of his mistresses. The listeners enjoyed the eavesdropping.

Not because the conversation was of any value, but simply because the words were a little spicy and naughty. Besides, they didn't need any new information about their infamous suspect. Their source had provided all the intelligence they needed to be able to finally put Vittori in a federal prison for good.

A cell phone rang in the lead van. The caller simply said to the agent who answered, "Go!" It was confirmation that Santino and Sittinz had been taken into custody in Coeur d'Alene.

Twelve crack FBI agents stormed the mansion. Each wore a dark blue coat with the letters FBI clearly visible. They covered every possible exit from the house. Two FBI helicopters instantly appeared overhead. The powerful beams of their searchlights illuminated the grounds. Four unmarked FBI cars with red lights flashing clogged the street in front of the mansion.

The four agents stationed at the front door broke it open with a steel battering ram. "FBI," shouted the first agent as loud as he could. The team took a hard right and headed directly for the library. They knew exactly where they were going. The blueprints of the mansion they studied were perfectly accurate and made their search a simple one. Two agents ran through the library door and the remaining two stood guard with their backs to the library entrance, their handguns drawn. Eight other agents entered the house from three other locations to secure the residence from top to bottom.

"FBI. Don't move! Vincente Vittori, you are under arrest," yelled the agent who had his weapon pointed right between the Don's eyes. Vittori didn't move a muscle or say a word for several seconds. He was frozen by the appalling surprise of it all. He was seated in a bright red oversized leather chair holding the phone to his ear with his right hand. He slowly replaced the phone handset in its cradle. The second agent handcuffed him and the two of them, hands gripping Vittori's arms, led him straight to one of the unmarked vehicles.

Vincente Vittori fumed and spit as they shoved him into the rear seat of the FBI vehicle. "Get your filthy hands off me." He wished he had Santino's switchblade to stick in their cursed bellies. Better yet, he wished Santino was there to do it for him.

The door slammed shut and Vittori was alone with his thoughts. *How did the FBI get to me? What about Santino? Why didn't Santino call? Is it possible he was caught red-handed and gave me up to save his own skin? Did he really shack up in Chicago or was that just a heretic's made-up story?* Vittori sat humiliated in the custody of the FBI.

Santino would never betray me. He wouldn't, would he?

The mansion's butler was immediately on the phone to Cordero but it was already too late. The FBI had planned a perfectly timed attack.

Cordero was snuggled asleep in his bed when the agents crashed through the door to his master bedroom. He was whisked out of his condo still wearing his satin pajamas.

At the same moment the FBI arrested Vittori and Cordero in Buffalo, another highly trained FBI team moved on Douglas, Demerelli and Stone in Coeur d'Alene. Two agents, both males, sat at the west side of the bar in Whispers talking to the bartender and drinking straight ginger ale with a squeeze of lime. In the lower section of the quiet bar, next to the south windows, a romantic couple sat drinking Irish coffee without the Irish. She was a tall attractive Native American descendant of the proud Kootenai Tribe of Idaho. Lolanne Flatika was the lead agent in this operation and she sat with her make-believe escort, also an FBI agent.

The defense team was seated in their usual seats in their victory garden. Douglas sat in the love seat looking through the flames and was flanked by his two associates. They were whispering amongst themselves so as not to be overheard by the lovebirds seated behind them.

Flatika's had a small listening device in her left ear.

Jack Bradley was still at the console of his secret surveillance operation. He watched the monitors showing the hallways of the penthouse level. The instant he saw Santino and Sittinz being escorted to the elevators, Bradley reported, "Okay Lolanne, they're under arrest and moving."

On her signal, the agents moved into action. The two agents at the bar got up and walked to the lower section of Whispers. At the same time, the loving couple downed the last gulp of their Irishless coffee and left their table as if they were departing. Flatika took some cash out of her wallet and dropped it on the table to pay the bill and play out the act.

The four arrived at opposite ends of the victory garden at the same time. They stood tall completely surrounding the defense lawyers. It took several seconds for the preoccupied barristers to notice they had company.

Demerelli was the first to look up. "What the hell do you people want? Can't you see we are having a private conversation? Beat it."

"FBI. You're under arrest for jury tampering," announced Flatika.

"What? We're attorneys, not criminals," argued Stone. Douglas said nothing.

"We know," said Flatika, not knowing which moniker was worse. The agents pulled the attorneys to their feet, handcuffed them right in the middle of their victory garden, and read them their rights.

Douglas, Demerelli and Stone were in shock. Never, in their worst nightmares, did they fear the FBI would arrest them. Their fears always centered on their client in Buffalo.

How did they know? wondered a half-intoxicated Douglas as they were led away. *How in holy hell did they know?*

CHAPTER THIRTY-THREE

KOOTENAI COUNTY COURTHOUSE

The Kootenai County Courtroom was packed with public, press and politicians. The anticipation in the room was electric. The jury bailiff opened the door to the jury room and twelve somber-faced men and women filed into the jury box and took their seats. The prosecutors sat at their table and carefully watched the jury as they entered. Sittinz was alone at his defendant's table. His now-defunct defense team was busy fending off their own gnarly legal problems. The judge had ruled it was okay for him to be without counsel because all the legalities of the case were concluded and the only remaining portion of the trial was the jury's decision. There could be no additional legal arguments and there were no more defendant rights to be protected. Plus, given the fact this case was being tried, for the first time in American history, under the Tribunal Order of the President of the United States, there could be absolutely no appeal.

Jacob, the courtroom bailiff, bellowed the grand entrance of the judge. For the final time, all rose. Judge Roger Hammond picked up his gavel before sitting at the bench. The judge looked Sittinz directly in the eyes, looked down at the gavel then slammed it down just as hard as he could. "Court is in session." He surveyed the courtroom. "Members of the jury, have you reached a verdict?"

The jury foreman slowly stood. He was more composed than when he spoke before but, nevertheless he was still quite nervous. "Yes, your honor ve have done dis. Yes."

"Bailiff, will you please present the jury's written decision to the Court?"

The bailiff did as instructed. The Court read the verdict himself. His eyes widened, seemingly expressing surprise.

The lead prosecutor was in on the Nikki Fargo blackmail attempt. He paid close attention to the judge's eyes while he read the verdict.

It's not possible they had another juror under glass, is it? wondered the prosecutor.

Judge Hammond looked at the jury and, one by one, asked each one of them if a verdict had been reached. Each indicated they had, in fact, reached a verdict.

"Why is he polling the jury like that?" asked a worried assistant prosecutor.

"I'm not sure, unless it's part of the tribunal process. It seems highly unusual," said chief prosecutor Hart.

The judge seemed a little confused. He read from some notes he had brought with him into the courtroom. "I am now asking the jury to give the Court the sentencing form. Whether there is a sentence or not does not matter. The Court must have both the verdict and sentencing forms in front of it before the defendant is charged or released."

The courtroom bailiff made his second trip from jury foreman to judge and handed the document to the Court. The judge looked at the paper and turned it over to look at the other side. He turned it to the original side again. Nothing was written on it. The judge looked at the jury and seemed mystified.

The prosecutors squirmed in their chairs. His honor returned both sheets of paper to the bailiff and sent them back to the foreman. The Court wrote down something on the remaining papers in front of him. Judge Hammond looked up and over to the jury with a funny look on his face. "Mr. Foreman, will you please read the verdict?"

Was it to be guilty or not guilty? The jury foreman took the papers from the bailiff and put on his reading glasses, which he had been nervously holding in his hands. The lenses were filthy with finger marks. The foreman looked at both pieces of paper and finally determined which one he should read first.

The courtroom was silent.

"His honor," fumbled the foreman, "I mean your honor, ve are the jury and ve have found dis defendant, Curtis Sittinz," he continued stumbling over the words and was now visibly shaking, "NOT." The Foreman had momentarily lost his place on the verdict form as he struggled to read through the thumbprints on the lenses of his glasses.

The *NOT* seemed to suck the air out of the courtroom. Sittinz began to smile. The prosecutors couldn't believe their ears. Even the normally stone-faced bailiffs had baffled looks. How could such a thing happen? The prosecution had clearly proven guilt beyond any doubt.

"It's that son-of-a-bitch Willy the car dealer," said Hart's senior assistant as he pushed his chair back from the prosecutor's table and put his head in his hands. "I knew it. They got to him and bought him off like a cheap whore."

The shock of it all struck Hart and he looked away from his pained associate toward juror William Payton. Willie stared back with no emotion.

The foreman gained his composure. "Yes, I'm sorry, here it is, I wrote it down myself," said the foreman still shaking. "Ve find him NOT innocent!"

Not innocent, thought the defendant. When he realized what had just been said, the smile on his face vanished and his head drooped down. He covered his face with his hands.

The public was temporarily confused. The judge clarified, "Mr. Foreman are you saying the verdict is guilty?"

"Yes, honorable judge. Dat is exactly vat I just said."

The public in the courtroom broke into cheers and the judge let it go on for a few seconds before gaveling order back into his court. The prosecutors slapped each other on the back and rocked back in their chairs with big grins. The bailiffs let out brief uncustomary smiles.

"Order please! Order in the court," shouted the judge as he pounded his gavel.

It took a minute or so, but the courtroom finally calmed down. Next to come was the tribunal jury's sentence.

"Mr. Foreman, the Court is confused by your sentencing form. Could you please explain why there is nothing written on the paper?"

"Nothing on de paper? Vat do you mean? Sure der is." He looked at the sentencing form he had sent the judge. It was blank. He rifled through the papers in his hand. "Oh, dear judge, I have mistaken. I gave you the paper I plan to use to write my grocery list for ven I go home tonight. I am a vidower and I must stop by the store. Here is the right form." He held it up for the Court to see. "It says life in prison vith no possible paroling."

The courtroom burst into applause and cheers again. This time the judge let it go a little longer. The courtroom bailiff transported the proper sentencing form to the Judge, so he could read for himself.

"Order, please!"

Reporters ran from the courtroom to call in the sensational story.

The Court stared down at Curtiz Sittinz. "Bailiffs, please remand convict, Curtis Sittinz, to the custody of the Federal Penitentiary System of the United States of America for the rest of his miserable life!"

CHAPTER THIRTY-FOUR

COEUR d'ALENE

Special Agent Lolanne Flatika sat at a table with Chief Prosecutor James Hart in an interrogation room at the FBI office in downtown Coeur d'Alene. They awaited the arrival of Anthony Cordero who was being brought to Coeur d'Alene for further questioning.

"It's been quite a roller coaster ride," Hart said.

"I would say so," she replied. "What was the deal on the car salesman? You know the mysterious phone calls and all."

"Turns out Willy has a habit of placing illegal bets with an underground bookie who evades police by changing his phone numbers and rerouting his calls every day or so. It's no big deal, but it put a hell of a scare in us for a while. Willy's being very co-operative and the local authorities will handle it from here."

The door to the interrogation room opened and there stood Anthony Cordero, attorney for Don Vincente Vittori. Two somber agents brought him into the room and sat him down on a chair between Flatika and Hart. It had been three days since Cordero was arrested. He was nervous and sweat beaded on his forehead and upper lip.

"Of course, you are well aware that Curtis Sittinz has been found guilty in the Emrae International scandal and the three attorneys you hired to defend him have been charged with jury tampering aren't you?" asked Special Agent Flatika.

"I am."

"Do you have any additional information you can provide regarding the defense attorneys' efforts to interfere with the jury in the Emrae case?" she asked.

"Not that I recall."

"Since the night of your arrest, we have kept you in isolation. You should also know that we have arrested your client, Vincente Vittori. He will be charged with his complicity in the Emrae affair and also murder."

"Murder? Are you sure about that? Do you really feel you have sufficient evidence to bring such a charge?"

Prosecutor Hart chimed in, "We're sure of it for two reasons. Vittori's henchman Santino was caught red-handed attempting to murder Curtis Sittinz by throwing him off an eighteenth floor balcony at the Coeur d'Alene Resort."

"But you stopped him before he was able to carry out the murder, right?"

"Yes," said Flatika.

"So, that is attempted murder, not murder. Has Santino told you he was under orders from Vittori?"

"No."

"So, how does that tie Vincente Vittori into murder?"

"Well, by itself it may not," said Hart. "However, the wire you wore on our behalf in Buffalo getting Vittori's own voice ordering the Sittinz hit absolutely proves the case!"

Anthony Cordero was working undercover for the FBI for over a year. He was caught on tape, himself, discussing illicit Emrae investments with Curtis Sittinz and Andrew Bronson. He was a little fish in the grand scheme of things but nonetheless he was swimming in the same murky pond as the rest of them.

Cordero realized he could never survive prison and turned state's evidence before the Sittinz trial had even started.

"Mr. Cordero, your help has ensured that we have all the evidence we need to deal with Vincente Vittori once and for all," said Special Agent Flatika. "For the last twenty years we have known he was the mastermind who planned and ordered scores of illicit criminal activities but he buffered himself so well we could never get to him. We couldn't even charge him with jaywalking."

"The only jaywalking he'll be doing from now on is back and forth across the prison exercise yard," said the prosecutor. "You've finally given us the direct link we needed."

"Even before you began cooperating with us, we had a pretty fair idea that Vittori and his gangster friends had their fingers in Emrae International's pie," said Flatika. "Wearing that wire took great courage."

Cordero grimaced as he thought, *if they had picked up on that wire I'd already be down there with Bronson.*

"The evidence you captured on tape guarantees Don Vincente Vittori will vacation for the rest of his life in one of the federal government's finest hotels. He's probably too old to survive even the minimum required sentencing for the Emrae thing," stated the prosecutor. "Now, with the little party he planned for Sittinz at the Resort, we've got him for sure."

"What happens to the defense attorneys?" asked Cordero.

"Oh, yes," smiled the prosecutor, "our three amigos, Douglas, Demerelli and Stone. Their little jury-tampering capers with juror thirty-nine's poor mother and Niki Fargo will cost them a few years. They'll live to see the light of day outside of the big house, but their days as barristers are over."

Flatika quickly added, "We had our sights on Santino the entire time he was with the poor little lady with Alzheimer's. If he had tried to harm one little hair on her head, we would have moved in and fast." Cordero's heart warmed to the thought that his authorization call to get the go ahead to briefly kidnap the old lady, was made not to Vittori, but the FBI. He also tipped the FBI to the fact that the defense would rest early if they were convinced that Nikki Fargo was on the jury.

"We're going to keep our word and leave Nikki Fargo's blackmail story sealed in the records of the Court. Her little trist will forever remain a private affair."

"What about Santino?"

Special Agent Flatika flashed a broad smile. "Vittori's little triggerman is in a major heap of trouble. We've got him on attempted murder, for sure. In addition, it seems the young hooligan that Santino recruited to steal the purse in San Francisco was an eyewitness to the murder. He was hiding behind a car parked in the garage not twenty feet from the scene of the crime. He saw Santino stab Michael Sanderson to death. The San Francisco PD didn't believe the kid, at first. After talking with us, they showed him a picture of Santino and he identified him as the killer. Santino's had his third strike. You don't have to worry about him."

For the first time in the meeting, Cordero smiled. He could now take comfort in the fact he had turned his own life around and played a major role in bringing a heinous crime family to justice. His office had made arrangements for the defense lawyers to stay at the Resort during the trial and even paid their hotel bills. It was natural, then, for Cordero to communicate with the FBI through Jack Bradley.

"Now it's time for you to excuse yourself, Mr. Hart, so we can finish our business with Mr. Cordero," said Flatika.

The prosecutor excused himself and as he left, a man Cordero had never met before entered the room. "Anthony Cordero, I would like you to meet Mr. Philip Nester. He is in charge of the witness protection program for the Criminal Division of the United States Department of Justice. He will be your contact. You will be safe in his care. To ensure the highest possible security, I will leave you two alone to discuss the details. The story the Bureau will tell is that somehow you gave us the slip. Nobody even knows we arrested you. You ran just like Sittinz and Bronson and, even as good as we are, we just can't seem to find you."

The Special Agent sensed earlier that Cordero wasn't sure if he was a traitor or hero by turning state's evidence. "They say when a person dies, his tombstone has two dates on it with a dash between them. The first date is when you are born and the second is when you die. Neither date is really very important. What's important is the dash between them. It is what one does during that dash that defines a person. The first Anthony Cordero's dash would have been badly tarnished. The brave actions of the second Anthony Cordero, or whatever your new name will be, has polished that dash and wiped the tarnish away. Your dash will represent decency and honesty."

"Thank you, Agent Flatika," Cordero said.

"No. On the contrary, thank you, Mr. Cordero for doing the right thing. Good luck, and take comfort in the courageous role you played to help bring about Infinite Justice!